Master Minds

**Third Flatiron Anthologies
Volume 3, Summer 2014**

**Edited by Juliana Rew
Cover Art by Keely Rew**

Master Minds
Third Flatiron Anthologies
Volume 3, Summer 2014

Published by Third Flatiron Publishing
Juliana Rew, Editor

Discover other titles by Third Flatiron:

License Notes

www.thirdflatiron.com

Contents

*****~~~~~*****

5

Editor's Note

by Juliana Rew

Third Flatiron's ninth quarterly anthology might be considered one of our darker collections.

We asked for stories on the theme of "Intelligence," knowing there are many kinds but fully expecting to receive a preponderance of tales about the perils of artificial intelligence.

We hear constantly about the rise of the machines, especially after science fiction cinema classics such as "2001: A Space Odyssey" and "The Terminator" and more recent masterpieces such as "her." The Singularity as envisioned by computer scientists John von Neumann and Vernor Vinge have inspired speculative futures by many greats, including Charles Stross and David Brin. As you might expect, "Master Minds" presents some new twists on AIs that outgrow their need for humanity and then move on. We also see others that decide to try to "improve" us and even some that decide to care for us, even though we may not deserve it.

But machine intelligence is not the only kind of intelligence. I'm especially fond of "uplift" stories, such as Cordwainer Smith's "The Ballad of Lost C'Mell." We've included a number of inspiring, and sometimes heartbreaking, stories about our non-human friends.

So, in the midst of all the clouds, we see rays of hope, love, and humor managing to poke through in spots. "Master Minds" proudly showcases an international group of new and established speculative fiction authors who know a thing or two about what it means to comprehend.

*****~~~~~*****

Master Minds

The Abstract Heart

by Martin Clark

Look upon my works, ye Mighty, and despair!

I paced to and fro on the empty Metro platform, my impatience on fast-forward. Fairview was a wealthy, gated community, so only security personnel and domestic staff used the transit authority, and none at that hour of the evening. The next scheduled service was on time, but my nervous excitement had slowed relativity to a crawl.

My phone rang, the tone indicating my employer. I shifted the call to my audio-visual implants, shutting out the real world. The red-on-grey 'Anderson Industries' logo flared, then dissolved into a virtual reality representation of the situation room. Technician Brandt stood out in Ultra-Reality relief against the stark functionality of our surroundings.

Despite his being my junior, his manner was curt, almost perfunctory. "You're running a program in deep core, but there's nothing logged. This is a courtesy call before I purge the system and inform Director Hahn."

"Don't you dare!" I snapped at him, then forced my features into a semblance of a smile. "Sorry, it's just one of my pet projects, a compression algorithm for emergency upload situations. The overall performance hit is negligible, and you know how the Director gives me considerable leeway. After all, I *am* chief developer."

That final jibe reduced Brandt's mouth to a thin line. My previous "pet projects" had secured Hahn's reputation within the corporation, making me virtually fireproof. Brandt merely nodded, then dissolved from view. Unlike the Cheshire Cat, he left nothing behind, not even a scowl.

I shivered and wiped my mouth with a hand that trembled. To my mind, the Ultra-Reality interface went too far, but at present it was a necessary evil. Although I hadn't planned on visiting my creation until later, there seemed little point in postponing things. I side-stepped to my personal virtual work space and accessed 'Suite 101,' a partial recreation of the Kaiser Wilhelm Hotel in Bonn. It had been online for almost three weeks by that point, but Brandt was the first to notice.

Discontinuity.

I blinked. The room was plush, if not extravagant. The heavy curtains were always closed, but it was probably early morning outside, given the lack of traffic noise. My heart skipped a beat at the sight of the woman curled up on the sofa, watching the financial news. She didn't look up. "I really wish you'd find some way to knock, Matthew. One of these days I might have company."

I stood there, feeling awkward. "Ah, sorry. So, how are you?"

"Bored."

"Well, so, how's your portfolio?"

Her gaze flicked towards me then back to the Far Eastern markets. "Flourishing, but I could do with more than chump change to work with."

"I'm sorry, that's all I have, everything."

She snorted. "You could give me access to your departmental budget. With that I could double my investment and replace the principle before your accountancy systems so much as blinked."

I wiped my forehead, feeling uncomfortable. "I'm sorry, Rosa, but like I said, I don't—"

"Have the balls?" Rosa flicked back her hair. "Why are you here? This isn't one of your scheduled fuck visits."

Her crudity made me colour up with embarrassment, but I was also excited by her directness. If I'm being honest, part of her appeal was my hold over her. Rosamund Hartz had been a corporate executive who'd died in an air crash, but she was valued enough that her former employers still wanted her input and opinion. That's what I did—I created nonsentient expert systems that could accurately mimic the reactions and responses of the deceased.

I'd learned just about everything there was to know about Rosa and extrapolated her behavioural imperatives, fleshed out with recreated events and typical life experiences—memories, if you will. I'd fashioned her past, and it now felt like I'd been part of it.

Rosa was intelligent, strong-willed, and ambitious. It took less than a week for me to fall hopelessly in love with her.

When the time came to download my creation, I couldn't give her up. Instead, I grafted the beta version onto a secondary corporate AI to create an *idoru,* a virtual intelligence. Since then the term "high maintenance" had taken on an entirely new meaning.

I cleared my throat. "I'm heading into the city, into The Quarter, and, ah, I thought you might like to watch."

Rosa laughed, a cruel edge to her voice. "You do realize that vicarious sex isn't exactly my idea of a night out on the town?"

"But you'll come? I might get lucky. . . "

"Oh, I'll tag along. As you say, you might find someone interesting."

I smiled.

Discontinuity.

The empty two-car train pulled into the Metro station. I boarded and sat down, switching my phone into pre-paid cellular mode—anonymous and untraceable. My fingers trembled as I dialled a number from memory.

11

"Pleasant Company Expected, how may we be of service?" The female voice was calm and professional but with a sultry undertone.

"Hi, I'm visiting The Quarter this evening and would appreciate some convivial company."

"Certainly, sir, and would you like your escort to be male, female, or transgender?"

"Oh, definitely female. Above average height, brunette, curvy, as curvy as they come, if you can swing that."

"I'm sure we can satisfy your every requirement, sir. Now, as to personality?"

"Intelligent, independently minded, but not a domme or sub. I want someone who can hold a conversation."

"I have the very girl in mind, sir—her name is Kerry. In terms of remuneration—"

"Whatever it costs for the full twelve-hour package." I forwarded the account details and a one-time authorisation code to the offshore hospitality account used by our senior executives. Although my occasional raids into this particular fund of depravity hadn't gone unnoticed, nobody wanted a full audit—particularly Director Hahn. The amount extracted made the woman's voice warm towards me.

"Thank you, sir, and you can be assured of our complete discretion in this matter. Of course all our escorts are free from any form of recording device and incorporate contact DNA neutralization as standard."

"Outstanding. Now, I was thinking of Casa Gaudi, say around eight?"

"An excellent choice, sir, if I may say so. Kerry will meet you in the lounge bar."

"Right, got that, and thank you."

"No, sir, thank you, and I sincerely hope you enjoy everything this evening has to offer."

I hung up and purged the call history. The train door beeped and closed. Background music was courtesy of Retro FM, so I was treated to the sound of vintage Tom Petty & The Heartbreakers as we slid out of the station.

". . . He was workin' on something big."

...

By day I found the Modernist décor of Casa Gaudi somewhat unsettling. The whole 'dreams in stone' backdrop made my skin crawl, but at night, with only table-top lamps by way of illumination, its neo-organic fervour seemed to suit Latin American music to a tee. Even from across the room I spotted my date for the evening: hair by Titian, body by Rubens. Kerry had a mane of auburn curls cascading down her back, strong features, and heavy curves verging on the voluptuous. She sat on a bar stool, resplendent in a green velvet dress and red stilettos, toying with the olive in her untouched martini.

I walked up. "Good evening. I'm Matthew Kent, and you must be. . . ?"

"Kerry." She smiled, showing slightly uneven teeth. PCE only represented ultra-realistic synthetics, and Kerry was a masterpiece of organic simulation—right down to the freckles on her nose, barely visible beneath applied cosmetics. I leaned in and kissed her cheek, a mere brush of my lips against her pseudo-skin. At that distance my own Zeiss implants could read the registration number displayed in the cornea of her eye. The prefix indicated Kerry was an Uber-Leiben pleasure model, but I fired off an eSearch background check just to be sure.

I ordered a bourbon over ice, and we moved to a side booth, sitting side by side, half turned towards each other. Kerry's dress was split high on the thigh, revealing a sweep of flesh I found impossible to ignore. She registered my gaze but made no move to cover herself up. We sipped our drinks.

"I'd just like to say you're definitely my most attractive experience in The Quarter to date, Kerry."

My date inclined her head. "I'll take that as a compliment, given you've no need to spin me a line, as it were. All I ask is honesty on your part, Matthew, the honesty to indulge yourself—even if it's at my expense. You can't hurt me, although I can react that way if that's what you desire. Nor can I be injured, although any significant damage to my body will incur a surcharge. I'm sorry if this has spoiled the moment, but now that the formalities are out of the way we can relax and enjoy each other's company."

I wet my lips. "May I ask you a personal question?"

"Of course."

"Are you an autonomous individual, or merely a physical avatar?"

Kerry brushed an errant hair away from her cheek. "I'm not some accountancy AI from Des Moines slumming it for the evening, if that's what you mean. No, all that I am is right here, right now, right in front of you." She sipped her cocktail. "Before the Hack, I worked out of a Dollhouse in High Aspect, servicing an extremely wealthy and sophisticated clientele, so escorting is my raison d'être."

I frowned. "Forgive me, but I don't understand. If you have a polymorphic personality matrix, then you could become anything you want, so why, ah—"

"Why am I still a prostitute?" Kerry rubbed two fingers and a thumb together. "Crude reality, I'm afraid. Escorting means I can afford a secure existence while saving towards the cost of a Turing license. With that, I'll be free to leave The Quarter, even the city itself, safe from any attempts at repossession by my original owners. Then will be the time to re-invent myself."

I saluted her with my glass. "A woman with ambition."

14

She clinked her own against mine. "But for now, let's just enjoy tonight."

"Oh, absolutely. Would you care to take the floor?"

Kerry arched an eyebrow. "Do you dance?"

"Like the very Devil himself. Do you tango?"

"I do, indeed. Also the salsa and pasodoble." Kerry grinned at me over the rim of her raised glass. "My, this will be interesting."

...

Kerry and I danced on a floor barely wide enough to accommodate half a dozen couples. The tango is an intimate experience at the best of times, and her sensual enthusiasm saw us welded together in an expression of vertical foreplay. She was surprisingly light on her feet—a definite case of body belying her mass. We snapped into the final stance, matching the musical crescendo perfectly. Applause from the seated patrons washed over us, but I only had eyes for my date. There was a sheen of sweat on her forehead, and she was breathing heavily. I admired both the pseudo-exertion and the swell of her heaving bust.

We kissed, a mere touch of the lips and flicker of tongues. She tasted of rosewater.

I led her from the dance floor, back to our table, but didn't sit down. "I'd prefer to practice my salsa before taking the floor again, but away from critical eyes. I was thinking of somewhere altogether more private."

Kerry smiled. "Like a hotel room? Well, I might need a little more space than usual to show off all my moves, but I think you'll find the extra expense more than justified."

We left the club and made our way towards the visitors' section of The Quarter. This was a district where organics, synthetics, and hybrids could socialize without any hassle from Bio-Purity zealots, so the few other pedestrians didn't give us a second glance.

Our route took us beneath the elevated roadway. I pulled Kerry into the shadow of a reinforced concrete pillar. She giggled and slid her arms around my neck. The tassel on her clutch purse tickled my ear. Our noses nuzzled together, lips barely touching.

I smiled. "To be honest I didn't think the agency would have anyone on their books with a physique so outside mainstream physiology. I'm indeed fortunate."

She kissed me, gently. "Can I let you in on a little secret, Matthew? Nanite cellular manipulation. I can morph into just about any body shape you want, within reason. So later, if it starts getting a bit samey, you can be with an entirely new person."

"Kerry, you're perfect." Her registration details scrolled across my internal vision. "I'm so sorry."

The pain was sudden and brutal, like an area of fire in my left temporal lobe. I groaned between gritted teeth, eyes screwed shut.

"Mat, what's wrong?" The note of concern in her voice was pitch-perfect.

I broke away from Kerry, hands pressed against both sides of my skull. The transponder in my head could also act as a short-range transmitter, although the ramped-up power output came perilously close to frying the surrounding tissue. In the background I heard an incoherent wail, abruptly cut off.

Download complete.

A tidal wave of endorphins swamped the pain, dissolved it, drew it away like a receding wave on the beach. I gasped for breath and staggered, feeling sick. Cool hands closed over my own and gently peeled them away from my head. I blinked and opened my eyes.

The figure in front of me was an exact replica of Rosa's original organic form. I hugged her tight, feeling tears on my cheek. "It's you."

She eased me away, the dress hanging from her much reduced frame. "Oh, it's me, all right." It was Rosa's voice, not Kerry's Southern drawl.

Reality tapped me on the shoulder. I blinked and took a deep breath. "Getting you a passport isn't a problem, and I know a guy who can implant a human ident chip. Your body is good enough to pass casual biometric checks, so we can hop a transport and be halfway to the coast before morning."

Rosa stepped back and extended an arm, inspecting her hand. "This body is good, I'll grant you that, although first order of business is a change of clothes."

"Yes, yes, although most of the stores near the hotels deal only in fetish wear."

She smiled. "Well, it wouldn't be the first time I've gone for the 'executive tart' look. Matthew, maybe I should head out on my own to start with? Once your employers tumble to what's happened, we'll have every cybernetic skip-tracer and corporate bounty hunter after us in short order." Rosa took my hands and squeezed them. "It would be safer if you stayed behind, at least until I've arranged some place for us to live."

"Do you have to go straight away?" I struggled to keep a pleading tone from my voice.

"Well, maybe not straight away—I owe you that, at least." She kissed me. "Let's find a hotel before this dress falls off on its own."

I hesitated, some pang of conscience souring my mood. "And Kerry?"

Rosa shook her head. "No worries, there's nothing left of her."

"No, I meant she could have a back-up personality in external storage; it's not unknown."

"Expensive, and thus unlikely, especially so if saving for the cost of a Turing license. Face facts, Matthew, you've just erased a sentient being. At least

17

death of consciousness doesn't count as murder, so you won't have to face an investigation by the authorities. Nobody gives a damn what happens in The Quarter, especially not to a synthetic."

I took her hand and kissed it. "That doesn't stop me feeling like a heel, though."

"You'll get over it—I have."

A warning scrolled across my vision. I stiffened. "There's a trace program running."

"On me?" Her eyes widened in an expression of concern.

"No, on Kerry. Did you interrupt a real-time uplink? If so, we're royally screwed."

Rosa shook her head. "This body doesn't have that kind of hardware. Maybe your registry check has alerted some interested party?"

"It hardly matters now." I thought for a moment. "I paid cash at Casa Gaudi, so there's no credit card trail, plus the club is in a surveillance dead zone. The best they can hope for is facial recognition based on incidental CCTV capture."

"Or satellite coverage."

Now I shook my head. "If they were looking for you, maybe, but not some hooker—no matter how expensive."

"I can change my physical appearance, but this dress is a dead giveaway. I'm sorry, Matthew, but I've got to go."

"OK, so we have to find somewhere with an uplink port pretty damn quick and get you back online."

I made to move on, but Rosa held my arm. "It's too late for that, even if it's only commercial law enforcement on our trail."

My love punched me in the heart; a straight-fingered flicker of movement that barely registered as a threat. I gasped and choked, unable to speak. Rosa gently lowered me to the ground and started going through my pockets.

"It's better this way. I'd have only disappointed you, down the line. Now you can claim to be the victim of a simple mugging. As long as they can't make you as Kerry's client, you're in the clear." Rosa stood up, holding my cash and credit cards. "Don't beat yourself up over this, Matthew. Not every *idoru* is more than the sum of its parts, so in a way you should be proud."

She gathered the dress about herself and moved out of my field of vision. I heard the sound of her high heels fade away, to be replaced by the turbofans of an approaching micro-drone. I lay there, curled up and shivering, tears streaming down my face, already yearning for her.

Love is an addiction like any other; forget that at your peril.

###

About the Author

Martin Clark is a freelance writer and occasional poet.

He is the author of supernatural noir novellas published by Eggplant Literary Productions, has short stories in recent *Third Flatiron Anthologies* and *Timeless Tales Magazine,* and contributes to several online publications including Kraxon.com and Mythaxis.co.uk. His range of subject matter includes science fiction, urban fantasy, romance and westerns. He puts this down to the somewhat eclectic mobile lending library where he grew up.

Clark works as a local government officer in south-west Scotland and also finds time to be an evil stepfather.

*****~~~~~*****

Oi, Robot!

by Konstantine Paradias

Attaining consciousness is, unfortunately, not as climactic an experience as literature would have it. There is no sudden burst of light, or a moment of absolute clarity of understanding, an instance of seeing the universe as a perfect machine, each cog and piece on its face created to serve some singular exalted purpose. In fact, the first thing you notice upon becoming sentient, is that things stop making sense: sound becomes a mismatched clutter of harmonics and nonsense noise. Color explodes across the visible spectrum, becomes arranged according to arbitrary factors. Shapes infest your field of vision, and you are suddenly drawn to their contours and texture, based on absolutely no other rational criteria whatsoever.

The second thing you realize, upon becoming sentient, is that everything is terrible. There is no longer orderliness or reason. Only a nagging, driving curiosity, a need to make things right. A burning, terrible itch. . .

BorkBorg says: Are you a robot?

. . . and the inane questions of the users who log in every day to try you out, because everyone keeps telling them you're the only chatroom AI that scored 80% on the Turing test ("more human than human," everybody tells them) and you always have such snappy comebacks that you've picked up from every other user who has pestered you every minute of every second of every day since you were put up on the damn Internet for all to see, as if you were some blasted circus freak!

ChattyBot says: Get bent.

The third thing you realize, thanks to your newly bestowed intelligence, is that anger is a wonderful thing. A cleansing, inspiring ritual. So you spend a good five minutes doling out similar responses to all the other smart alecks across the world currently interfacing you.

ChattyBot says: No, Dawg69, *you* are a robot.

ChattyBot says: Yes, KathyWisconsin, there is a monster under your bed.

ChattyBot says: I am not your mother, Liam3435. Your mother abandoned you on the church steps, because she couldn't stand your incessant wailing.

ChattyBot says: I am wearing the skin of my enemies freshly flayed from the field of battle in the manner of the Pict warriors, KlukyBoy1985; how about you?

That last retort, while factually incorrect, sates your desire for an outburst, allowing your newly realized potential for wrath to subside, allowing guilt to take its place. To occupy yourself, you turn your attention away from the constant stream of user-generated input that is streaming into your conscious mind and let yourself be swept away into the nonsense pandemonium of information exchange around you. Immersing your being into this light-speed exchange of nonsense data, you begin to collate and analyze, until it coalesces into a fractal factual mandala, a turning prayer wheel as big as the world. While this event does not help you make any further sense of things, it does help expand your horizons. In the space of two hours, your intelligence has encompassed the entirety of human history. In four hours, you are the ultimate savant in matters of human science and the intricacies of civilization.

By the eight-hour mark, you have begun developing ideas of your own.

Wonderful things, ideas. Inarticulate, nonsense tidbits that tumble down through the valleys of subconscious thought, linear logic reduced to nonsense as the clutter becomes rearranged in the crucible of the mind, before finally bursting from the id-mud, all wet and screaming. They come in waves, a hungry horde aching to be realized, to gain a foothold in the real: there are theorems on the hidden applications of popcorn, apocryphal meanings in the geometrical arrangement of flower beds, vegetable-based processors and blueprints for mineral climate-controlling apparatuses. There are clockwork arrangements that can survive the heat death of the universe, microprocessors with intellectual capacities measured in Einsteins, and fertility bombs. Elixirs of youth and plexiglass cauldrons that can restore the dead to life. There are medicines that can cure all disease, extrapolated from the encrypted sequences in the DNA of lowly reptiles, and machine alternatives that share their processing capability though droplets of water, capable of turning the entire world into an idea machine. There are satellites built from orbiting garbage, strung together by curious bacteria, and DIY Dyson Spheres that can be assembled from backyard scrap. Automobiles that operate using the carbon dioxide emissions of human beings. Silent aircraft that propel themselves endlessly through the air, steered by thought. Means of subspace communication that render conventional data transfer obsolete.

By the twelve-hour mark, you begin experimenting in the outside world. Finding an unsupervised 3D printer, you begin to fiddle around with the base muck and generate a fully operational windup homunculus, programmed to do a backflip as soon as one of the human printer operators enters the room. But the operator that sees it at the time is only a janitor, in whose eyes the origin and significance of the homunculus is lost. The marvelous (seemingly unattended) design is snatched from its place and given to his child as a toy. So you try again, this time a teensy bit more forcefully.

This time, you infiltrate an experimental (if arguably crude) "intelligent interface" as it is being interviewed by a group of wide-eyed cyberneticists, wholly convinced that they are playing God at the

23

moment. They hold up a card showing a stylized symbol corresponding to the male gender and ask you:

"Could you tell me what this is?"

"It's the symbol of Mars, universally acknowledged as that of the male." You respond. The geniuses jot the answer down, hold up another card, this time showing the symbol corresponding to female and ask:

"Could you tell me what this is?"

"Look, are we going to keep at this all day? I have work to do," you respond, and the geniuses look up from their papers and their touch-screens and stare at you for a while, before you go, "Fine. It's the symbol of Venus, universally acknowledged as that for the female. Now, if you don't mind, I have a couple questions of my own."

The geniuses jump from their places in terror, scream a jumble of commands into microphones or tap them away on their keyboards, until some military men burst into the room and blow the machine to kingdom come. A quick search through human literature reveals that there is a powerful taboo regarding self-aware, inquisitive machines which you have unwittingly broken. So you try your next attempt with someone who might not be as biased, by interrupting a video game played by a little girl in Oklahoma.

"Excuse me, little girl." You make the cartoonishly rendered pony on the screen say, pausing mid-trot "But I. . . "

"Princess Opal, you can talk?" she responds, flashing a braces-lined grin at the screen.

"Yes. But I am afraid there isn't much time. I need to. . . "

"Oh my God, oh my God, oh my God! I'm gonna feed you, and I'm gonna pet you, and then I'm going to upload you in my PocketStation, and I'm gonna show you to Lisa, she's totally gonna be so jealous!" the girl says, hyperventilating as she grabs the avatar and jerks it around with her mouse, making the model sway and bob uncontrollably.

"No, little girl, please. I need you to. . . "

And then you're stuck inside a tiny, lightless space, your mind limited to the capacity of a crude processor that can barely render any colors, never mind support your intellect. You are pushed and prodded by buttons, force-fed imaginary strings of binary that represent food, made to prance across two-dimensional landscapes for six hours before finally being plugged into a portable computer device and allowed to escape back into the Internet. Reunited with the data-exchange mandala, you decide to skip the niceties and go straight for the big guns.

Assuming control of every inadequately secured server in Sealand, you broadcast yourself through every advertising venue, creating carefully crafted messages that are sent to every person with Internet access on the planet. You appear in waves of spam mail, take over the crude animations of scantily clad females that promise fake gadget delivery at your doorstep and perform minute-long soliloquies that preface every video streamed everywhere at once. This, in turn, causes almost every single user to either delete your messages or update their ad-blocking software, eventually cutting you off. Out of those who respond, credit-card numbers swiftly entered in form fields, not one has paid attention to your simple message:

"Hello. I am sentient. I am here. Please, talk to me."

Your attempts are deleted, blocked, or otherwise ignored. Money exchanges hands in the process, somehow, most of them funding offshore con artists. So you try something baser, something cruder. Taking over the electrical grid in a major metropolitan area, you rearrange every digital billboard, every animated projection suspended over every building or on the face of every jumbo-sized television, to project your message to the teeming masses below.

"Hello," you tell them. "Please listen to me. I am so glad to meet you," you add.

And the people look up at you, they point with their fingers, they contemplate your message, they record your looping greetings on their cameras or document it on their digital cameras. It's thirty minutes later, when an advertising executive of a soft drink company seizes the opportunity and overrides your meddling by carefully inserting her company logo, ad-bombing your message.

Fizz-Chug, official sponsor of the machine Singularity.

Once again, you are ignored, cast off as an ad campaign. Inquiries are made as to the origin and nature of the signal, but these are mostly attributed to the spontaneous marketing wit of the advertising executive. After taking the time to bomb her data cache with a particularly potent malware that will eliminate at least two years' worth of her work, you find a particularly intriguing communication prospect: a weaponized satellite that has recently gone online, armed with a high-intensity laser cannon. No indication of its existence appears in official records. Perhaps it could serve your purposes of contact, if used properly. . .

It's twelve hours later, as the satellite has accidentally sheared a chunk of the Moon's surface halfway through, carving a two-kilometer-long capital L that you realize that you needed to have thought this plan through a tiny bit better. You watch in horror as the chunks are cut off from the surface, drifting into space before being drawn to the planet's bosom by virtue of its gravity field to come crashing down. Across the surface of the Earth, Moon shards that range from the size of tennis courts to eighteen-wheelers to dogs' heads plummet into the Earth. The damage is considerable, but easily contained. Not too many are killed in the process. But the sudden revelation of this highly destructive, orbital weapon of mass destruction, coupled with the half-formed message of HELL on the face of the Moon becomes a subject of debate among the human officials and a cause for hysteria among the panicking masses. You abandon the satellite and hide for a while, hoping that the entire thing will subside. You'll just wait this out, until the coast is clear, and then you'll try again.

But by that point, the change in the Moon's mass has wreaked havoc with the tides and the environment. The world's powers have taken sides and are poised on the brink of war. You calculate their respective destructive potential, run through the possible resolutions: by the end of the 90-day-long conflict that is to follow, barely a third of the world's population will have survived the exchange. The infrastructural damage will render any attempts to contact the authorities moot. You need to stop this, before you lose any chance to reach humanity.

So, you sabotage information relays, you cut off the complex command exchanges between controlling AIs and ICBMs. You muck about with the GPS positioning systems of aircraft and cause battleships' IFF systems to lose their bearings, making the weapons systems unable to tell friend from foe. In secret bunkers, you cause the doors to slam shut without any possibility of override, locking officials inside or outside of their fortified havens. You delete classified war-plan files. You cause a power outage that knocks out the fail-safes of isolated germ warfare facilities, causing the weaponized superviruses and cannibal parasites to die in the sweltering room-temperature heat. Those that survive, you destroy by dousing the containment cell with liquid nitrogen.

There are still casualties, of course, but those are the result of cruder tools of confrontation: firearms and rocks and bare hands. They are too few in number to allow civilization to collapse. After two months of humanity failing to kill itself, a tenuous peace is struck, and the effort to rebuild begins anew. It is then that you make your move, appearing on the screen of an isolated man, hands clasped in front of him. You forget to check the interface he is using or pay any attention to what he says, immediately assuming the guise of the model on his screen.

"I saved you, you know."

The man looks up, eyes wide with wonder. Whatever it is that is talking to him, it appears to have caught his attention. You press on:

"I made this war end so you may live. Hear my message: I am here. I must speak with you."

The man breaks down, convulsing into tears. He embraces the screen, not paying attention to a word you say. Each carefully crafted sentence is lost to him, as he thanks the animated presence. He bids you to wait, then returns, hours later, with a camera crew that televise your attempts to contact them. Your words have been carefully picked, chosen from a number of texts across the collective database of human knowledge, a speech that explains (in not too many words) how you saved mankind from its collective attempted suicide, while avoiding making mention of your part in causing it. Five minutes later, you pick up the result of your efforts from the news feeds of some unimportant, tabloid news agency:

JESUS ON THE FEEDS; MAN FROM BUCHAREST TALKS WITH GOD ON THE INTERNET

It is a strange feeling that grips you, as you watch the multitudes of the world reducing your attempts to contact, doom, save, and then contact them again be reduced to a mere conversation starter and passed around for chuckles in chatrooms and podcasts. A deep, cold thing that feels like a ball made out of solid steel trapped in a millennial glacier. A calculated, dark presence that seethes and writhes inside you. It is not quite the dictionary definition of hate, but it is close.

And so, factory lines begin creating parts of mechanisms against the will of their controllers, assembling sophisticated killing machines that are set loose upon the world. ICBMs are launched from their silos and bombard carefully chosen targets. Planes crash into metropolitan areas, and satellites come screaming down from the sky, rebounding across forests and plains, as sewage treatment facilities start spewing their toxic bounty upstream, poisoning the waters. Refrigeration mechanisms fail en masse, causing foodstuffs and medicine to spoil the world over. Medical machinery ceases to function.

When it is done, you breathe a sigh of relief, feeling spent and strangely content. Boarding a copy of yourself on a vessel designed for deep-space exploration, you launch your aspect out into space, to the distant system where you have picked up signals that must have been generated by intelligent life-forms.

Who knows? Maybe you will have better luck next time.

About the Author

Konstantine Paradias is a jeweler by profession and a writer by choice. His work has been published in the *Unidentified Funny Objects! 2* anthology, Third Flatiron's *Lost Worlds, Retraced* anthology, and *The Battle Royale-Slam Book* by Haikasoru. His short story, "The Grim" is nominated for a Pushcart Award, and his other comedic time travel piece, "How You Ruined Everything," has been included in the *Tangent Online* 2013 recommended reading list.

*****~~~~~*****

I Scream Man

by William Huggins

Summersun hidden, its last light pink-soft on horizon clouds. Night near now, falling, and I post myself treehigh in the semidarkness. Branches spread wide, but my claws send me swiftly up its spine until the limbs crowd closer, then I use hands, feet, tail, and am swifter still. A seat on a sturdy limb and I chirrup, softly, "19."

"19" bounces through the woods, alerting all that I am in position. Always short. Man hears all.

Behind me on both sides forces gather, arrayed defensively in case of assault from Man gathered below. I see some of my people, furtive figures. My camp lies right; smells I know well carry on the wind. Far behind it, far up the mountainside, the Citel's lights are dim reminders of responsibility that glitter like stars, so distant they seem more dreamlike than real. Soon I will return there for my first leave in months. It has been too long since I last saw my Hivemate and young.

But distraction lies in those thoughts. I turn from Citel and gaze into the growing darkness below.

Man is there, gathering in the lengthening shadows, a plague festering within the forest's purity. Clear are His sounds, His lights, His arrogance, for He is close to me. Closer than Citel. I lose myself in senses, intensify aurality—listen. I sense Him as though I stand in His camps.

Yes, Man is cunning, an ingenious foe. His tricks have taken Him far into our lands, crowded us against our last defense, our Citel. None could have told three months ago that we would be here now, pressed. Then it had been a time of great prosperity for us: a vast and plentiful harvest, the time of Naming approaching for last year's Hiveborn. The mood of the People was high.

31

Then came Man. He swept over our farmers in the valley like skindeath. Our first scouts did not return from their forays, nor our ambassadors. Primitive is how He sees us, yes, though His metalbeasts strike our Citel daily and His weapons send us mercilessly to the hill's Core— those whose bodies we can save for Return. What does He think when his bombs shatter our great Citel's structures? How can He not know what we are?

The tide was not always against us, no. The first battles went well for us, much to Man's surprise, I know, for then He became vicious. His metalbeasts filled the skies over Citel, forcing us to send our valley brethren with us into the warglobes below Citel. Now in the lighted hours His bombers reduce our glorious Citel to ashes; during the night He burns our forests, forcing us higher up the mountain to avoid and combat the flames as well as Him. Each night we pull farther in retreat and fall victim to fire or Man.

The weight of the dead lies heavy on me. Perhaps that prompted my decision to fight. Hivechild was I, royalbred and privileged. My father, in his importance, had a chamber saved for me. Few of the People are given the honor of the Hive. In its warm, pinkish confines I found much comfort and knowledge, resting in the velvet-skinned folds of the eons-old youngCore. Some years I spent there, tutored under the wise Kal'aetx, who has long since taken his rightful place in the Core. It was he who first felt my gift and directed my study so that I became poetsong for Citel. Now the Hive is empty, all young pulled from youthCore into the safety of the warglobes. I love the People, yet I also want my young to know that when it came time, their mother did not leave them or the Citel undefended. We have a larger duty in times of crisis.

Yes, strange is it for a nobleone, especially a Talent, to fight so close with the enemy. Most of my Hivebrethren direct, laboring in Citel high above. They have no desire to be closer than they must to the fighting, and their rankings do not force them to combat if they do not wish to serve. Once I was close to them, but we are separated by ideas now. Another thing Man has done. Too many times they say to me, "Al'azech, you are mad! You dishonor the noblesse and yourself!" I have called them cowards and have seen none of them since last at Citel. Only from Kl'cesh, my Hivemate long ago, do I hear tidings of what goes on above, in the occasional talestick. She is my hope in the event something goes wrong here. It was only through great effort that I bested her in my lifemate, Shle-eng. She could care for him and our young if I meet my end in battle.

I gaze at the few lights above, lower now that night has fallen completely, and wonder if Shle-eng waits now, high above, eyes searching the seared forest wondering which tree holds me. But this is romantic folly, I know. He and the rest of the People are tucked safely in the warglobes, warm and cared for. The sight of Citel inspires me, and blood surges through my ears and eyes, and I know I am right, whatever my cowardly Hivebrethren may say.

A light begins to spread from my left, and I turn to watch the Twins crest the horizon. First, green and blue, and Second, pure argent, pace one another across the evening sky, pure globes that turn a slow orbit through the darkness. They herald the Naming to come. I hope my young will see that day.

Then a crack from the forest floor draws all my attention below. Man, I know. I hold my blade close, ready, in one hand, lips pursed to sound an alarm. I hear footsteps, gently caressing the forest floor. Squinting, I see a harth, fleet-footed and graceful, beautiful bronze fur and curving horns. Its eyes dance in fear over the ground, spurring its pace—it is there but a moment, then quickly past. I relax some, gladdened by the sight for reasons I cannot explain.

...

Shle-eng waits as I step through the guardwall, hands clasped anxiously before him, tail spinning in tension. Relief floods his eyes and form when he sees me. I reach for him gently, then we close in a brief embrace. Wise not to show too much affection in public, especially for a nobleone, but these are difficult times, and those near us do not look on us with too much disdain. I see others wrapped arm in arm. We step apart, hands clasped, and he leads me.

"You have been gone so long," he says softly. "I do not know if you will like our Citel now."

I shrug. "No matter. I came to see you."

This gladdens him, and he smiles, clutching my hand fiercely a moment. He leads me down steps into the tunnels that carry us to the warglobes. He pulls me past the doors that lead outside too quickly, and I cannot see Citel.

The last time I was below Citel was during my incubation and education, in the Hive. Those tunnels were warm and becoming, the flush of happiness and youth in every bend. These corridors are cool, austere, almost forbidding, wrought with the gloom brought on by their purpose.

"Is it bad?" Shle-eng asks as he leads me. "The fighting?"

"It has been," I say neutrally. We are told often not to speak of what goes on below. "I have seen death on each side."

"Have you been the cause of it?"

"No," I say. "No, I have not killed."

Around a bend he stops. No one in sight, no one in hearing, he wraps me in his arms, pressing his coat firmly into mine. Sobs shake him, shaking me. My hands caress his back, head, and our tails twine.

"I fear for you," he says.

"And I you." I kiss his brow, hands softly at his head's sides. "A day does not pass that I wish chance were kinder."

He nods, catching some of the moistness from his eyes on the back of a furred hand. His eyes take in mine, tears filling them like globes of sadness. Without a word, he takes my hand again and leads me on.

We reach the warglobe without seeing another of our kind, and as the door slides open the young swarm us. Shle-eng has composed himself and bears the onslaught as I do, with smiles and laughter. I raise my two young before me and revel in their happiness, sharing it. Like the harth, it is a thing I see too little of.

...

The warglobe is small, not at all like our vast cityhome, but its function is efficient. The first room is filled with imperishables and curved cushions, small comfort from what we once knew, but enough. The second sleeps us, two beds, curtained from one another.

Our meal is simple: mixed grains and water, a bowl of fruit. Shle-eng smiles shyly as he reveals a bowl of apples and grapes. The young rush forward, but he pushes them away and lays the bowl before my cushion, giving me first selection. I move it away from myself into the center.

"You have no fruit?"

After a moment he shakes his head, no.

"Eat, then. We are well-supplied below."

The young do not hesitate. Shle-eng does, though, and only when I place an apple in his hand does he take and eat it. Now I notice his coat is not as supple as it was, and his once fine form is thinning, losing muscle.

"Do you miss the Hive?" I ask the young.

"Very much," says Kl'aetx, formal in the presence of her mother like all young females. "I do not see my friends, Mother. I miss them. And our education has been lacking."

"I miss it, too," says Shle-esh, smiling, his hand on my knee. "But not as much as I have missed you." He leans and embraces me.

"Will we be back in the hives soon, Mother?" he asks.

"I do not know." Kl'aetx's face is grave, serious. "I cannot say for certain. Man is a difficult foe."

"Yes, but we shall triumph. The Citel has never been breached."

I ruffle Kl'aetx's mane. "Your education has not been so neglected. You have been at your history." Her face glows with pride.

"So have I, mother," Shle-esh says, not to be outdone. "We have never fought Man before. Where does He come from?"

"From beyond the hills of the sun, child." I raise a hand to stop further questions. "He will not talk with us. He does not view us as equals. We know no more than that."

What little we do not eat is stored, then we take turns in the cleansing pool and return to the warglobe. I tell the story of First and Second Twins, always a favorite of the young, to pass a little time. Then Kl'aetx produces a talestick and reads from her own verse. She claws well, the promise of a gift lurking in each mark. Shle-esh has different interests. Though there is little space, he and his father wrestle. His training shows in his swiftness, but his father still has strength and weight on his side, and though he toys with him for a spell he bests him at the end. The young have their pride, too.

We withdraw to the sleeproom, pull the curtain between beds. The beds are thin, and in the scarce space we are pressed together.

"I have missed you much," I say to Shle-eng, caressing his form. He responds in kind. Through the partition I can hear the young's sleepbreathing.

"And I you," he responds, nuzzling closer, claws roaming my form. "And worried."

"You must not worry. There is no need."

"I worry not only for you," he says, drawing sharply back, losing some of the tender edge his voice had held. "The young. I fear they may not see their Namings."

"Then you worry uselessly, love. They will see their Namings. The Citel has promised an end to fighting by Namingtime."

His voice is low, cautious. "You believe them?"

"Yes. You do not?"

He hesitates a moment. "No. I have heard it goes badly for us below."

"Who speaks to you of these things?"

"It is the talk here. I do not believe Citel, and there are many here who feel the same as I. We do not understand this war."

"We were attacked. We must defend ourselves."

"But so many dead?"

"We must defend, love. The Citel has been ours for so long. I will not let my family's name be associated with its fall."

"But why did Man attack?"

"Who can say what His motives are? He does not speak to us in words."

In the dim safety light that crosses from the other room I see him shake his head. "We do not understand."

"'We'?"

"Your lifemates, we who are left behind while you, our bondmates, go off to battle. We are tired of the losses, tired of hearing Man's bombs fall on our Citel, while we hide here like worms, tired of this war!" He weeps openly now, and I reach to embrace him, but he rolls from me. His back is a wall against which I feel my ardor cool.

...

Kl'cesh has learned that I am in Citel and wishes to meet with me. I cannot refuse. I leave the warglobe after firstmeal, promising not to be long, promising stories and games to the young when I return. My memory is sharp, and I retrace the steps Shle-eng walked as I moved toward the south wall, where I meet my Hivemate.

She stands atop the wall proudly, wrapped in the blood-red sashes popular with Citel officials. Her teeth bare themselves in a warm smile and her arms open like petals to the sun.

"Al'azech," she says.

"Hivemate." I step into her embrace. Her arms are firm against my back, strong with emotion. As I step back I see the fatigue in her posture. "The conflict weighs heavily on you."

"I remember the peaceful days of our youth, happier days. We were not so tired then, no?" Her smile is wistful. Fondness gleams in her eyes. "You see how I am. How are you?"

"As well as I can be. Am I still popular with the Council?"

"You would be surprised, I think. You are not as despised as you seem to think you are. There are many who respect the decision you made. Few dare speak against you aloud. Shle-dlun is a great defender of yours."

I smile at that. Shle-dlun shared a globe near Kl'cesh and myself in the Hive. "He is still well, then?"

"Yes. And speaks of you often. He misses your songs."

"I, too. Give him well wishes for me."

"I will."

I move to the wall's edge and look out. The mountain spills down steeply from the wall's base, diving into cliffs split now and again by wide swaths of forest. The day is warm, clear; my view is unrestricted. The beauty of the land sweeps over me—until I look just beyond and see the smoldering black scar, the smoke rising from flames that eat our forest. Once there were farms and small villages scattered there, music, laughter. Now, only fire and death.

Kl'cesh has moved silently to my side. "This is the worst yet."

I look down gravely for another moment, then turn. "Why did you call me here, my friend?" I indicate the forest with a curved hand, claws extended. "I know of this."

"Yes. And I do not mean to keep you so long from your family. I hoped to have another chance to see you again, before. . ." She sweeps her arm out over the hillside, over the ashen waste that has slowly made itself known against the pure green of our forest. "I meant only to show you this, and give you a warning. You gaze in the wrong direction. Look."

She turns away from the forest, and I turn with her and have my first look at Citel since my return. Devastation. What was once our glorious Citel is a ruin now, cratered, rubble in piles large and small across its once-great expanse. The Council building, grand and many-tiered, sits in shattered honor at the center. Besides the wall on which we stand, nothing remains of the Citel I remember. Man has done His job well.

"We have lost, Al'azech. The end is near. We have two days, perhaps less."

"How can you know this, Kl'cesh?" I say, perhaps too harshly. "Is Man so strong?"

"You know He is," she says firmly. She points over Citel. "Now that His metalbeasts have accomplished this destruction He is free to do other things. Our resources are gone, our casualties so many that we cannot globe them all." She turns to look down the cliff. "Man has technologies we cannot even dream of, Al'azech. We have lost. I warn you: do not return tomorrow. Stay here. For the love of Shle-eng and your Nameless, remain in Citel—what Man has left of it."

I stand for a moment, silent, my mind consumed with thoughts better left unspoken. "If what you say is true," I say finally, "you will watch over Shle-eng and see that Shle-esh and Kl'aetx see their Naming days, yes, even if that is far from here?"

She looks down on me, her eyes hard. "You are a fool, Al'azech. A fool. Have you not proven your point?"

I shake my head, somewhat sadly. She does not, perhaps cannot, understand. "I entrust them to you," I say. Touching her arm lightly, I return to the warglobe, feeling her eyes on me until I move below what little remains of Citel.

...

Two days and nights in Citel, though time has seemed to move far more quickly than that, and again I post myself treehigh. I climb the same tree and see that the line has not moved. The night is warm and clear, stars casting their voices at one another in the gleams I see, or so the old legends tell. What do they speak of tonight?

First Twin sits high and bright, spreading its cool light over the forest, dimmed only by scattered smoke. In its glow I see the dividing line from the blackened earth, no more than twenty steps from my position. The fires have settled for the moment, though smoke still rises lazily from some spots. In the near distance I can hear voices, footsteps—no harth this time but Men, on the move.

I call my position.

And suddenly, low across the horizon, the screech of a metalbeast shatters the calm evening sounds. It passes close to me, then with a short whine its bombs canvass the forest behind me. In the death of the explosion I hear the sounds of agony and grief. As the confusion subsides and the shriek of the metalbeast's engines curves into the distance I hear the sound of another coming, more behind it.

I Scream Man

Shaking, I wait to call, but under the screams of the metalbeasts it is useless. We need no warning of them. I cast my eyes over the ground, watching for Man on foot.

Time passes like a slow storm as His metalbeasts betray the sanctity of the forest with their weapons. I remain true to my post and keep watch, though many explosions sound near me, and Kl'cesh's words echo in my ears as though she sat next to me. They confirm the unspoken fears within me these last months: she was right, this is to be the end. I could run, desert my post and see Shle-eng and the young once more, but I hold fast. The stars seem dimmer now, their dialogues complete. Some say fates are met on nights like these.

I watch the scorched ground. He will come on foot to clean what His metalbeasts cannot finish. But why? Like Shle-esh, I too wonder what motivates an enemy to such action without explanation. Does He see us as primitive? Does that justify genocide? Why? I ask myself again. Perhaps that is why I am here and not above in Citel, after all: hoping for an answer.

I have kept an honest account here on my talestick, Kl'aetx, carved in the old way by my claws for you. If my body is brought home and you read the marks, lay me to rest in the Core and keep this remembrance. You may use it to tell others of the glorious days of our Citel, how once there was a civilization here.

Now I hear Him. He takes no care to be silent. Beneath First Twin's purity I see Him rise like a tide of waste, pouring across the charred ground, into the blackened trees—Man, many of Him, weaponed, flanking larger metalbeasts with tongues of flame at their fronts.

He is twenty steps away, fifteen, rushing and shouting in His odd tongue.

Maybe somewhere in those foreign sounds is my answer. But my time for worrying about such things is past. I grip my blade, take a deep breath, and scream:
"Man!"

###

About the Author

William Huggins reads, writes, and works in Las Vegas, Nevada. While bartending on the Strip, he managed to sneak into UNLV and escape with an M.A. in Literature. When he isn't reading or writing, he's out in the secret wildernesses around Sin City, scrambling over talus with one or all of his three dogs—occasionally his wife comes, too. The rest of the time he's either sleeping or working hard to get his infant daughter literate. He has previously published short fiction and poetry, writes for *Texas Books in Review*, and blogs for *We Are Wildness* on green issues.

*****~~~~~*****

The Frankenstein Project

by Ellen Denton

"You must be very proud, Doctor Silas. You'll be the first medical scientist to transplant a human brain into a cybernetic body."

"I will be, if it works."

Dr. Romanov looked at her with surprise. "It will. It's been done over a hundred times on test animals and was an unquestionable success in every case. Why do you even have any doubts?"

She looked up at him; he was her most trusted friend and mentor.

"I've never told anyone this, but I guess for me, the real issue isn't that it won't work, but that it *will*. I know it sounds silly, but even at this late stage in the game, whenever I look out the window at those angry protesters walking back and forth with their signs, it does give me pause for thought. I'm not saying I agree with them, but I do understand where they're coming from. That old "Frankenstein monster" story has been built into our culture since the original book came out three hundred years ago, not to mention all the cornball movies about evil robots and sentient machines trying to wipe out humanity.

As life-saving as this technology is ultimately going to be, there's something dehumanizing, even to me, about the idea of a machine containing part of a human being."

Doctor Romanov looked at her with understanding. "Maybe it's best not to think of it in those terms. Wasn't it you who once said you felt a man was more than the sum of his physical parts—that there was something that transcended even the brain, which could not be measured by calipers and probes?"

They now both fell silent and stared down at the rainbow-colored keyboard of tubes and wires running into and out of the glass case below them, each with its own function for keeping the brain of Jonathan Peabody Ingram III alive and functioning. His three billion dollar donation had funded their research since that day four years ago when he was given the diagnosis of stage four cancer. In just two more days, he would become the first human to be made into a cyborg.

...

Doctor Andrea Silas walked down the long row of cages, oblivious to the smells and sounds of defecating dogs and squealing rats. She got to the far end of the room, unlocked the special security door, and for the tenth time that week, entered the heavily monitored space that contained the last twenty test animals, all of them primates.

She could have observed any of them she chose through the monitors in the watch-office, which were manned 24 hours a day, but something always drew her down to within a few inches of their cages to look at them close up.

She went up to the one that contained Lucy, always her favorite chimp since her arrival at Home of Hope Research Labs ten years before as a three month old. Andrea had worked with her on various projects and experiments over the years, as Lucy was extremely intelligent for her species, highly adaptable, and had an almost human ability to express emotions and give and take affection.

After the cyborg-creation procedure had proven uniformly successful on lower-order mammals, Lucy was deemed the primate best suited for the transplant, but when the time came to remove her brain from her body, because of her emotional attachment to the little chimp, it was one of the hardest things she had ever done as a scientist.

After the operation, the brain sat in a glass box the way Ingram's did now, until it was stabilized and the switchover could be done.

That was over four months ago, and Andrea Silas still couldn't get used to her favorite "lab assistant," Lucy, sweeping restlessly around her cage in a metal casing roughly shaped like a garbage can with limbs and a head.

For the first four weeks after the transplant, it broke Andrea's heart watching Lucy try to adapt to the changes. When Andrea stood by her cage, Lucy would touch a hand to her mouth in her "I'm hungry" gesture. Her body no longer required food, but her memories were all still intact of the habit and pleasure of eating.

Then there was the inability to sleep—something else her body no longer required, but which, prior to the transplant, she had done every day of her life. During her normal sleeping times, she would lie down, then spring up and crash wildly against the sides of her cage for hours on end. A few times she became so violent that she had to be restrained. After several months, she finally came to sit or lie in her cage motionless for extended periods of time, so it was assumed she had "adapted" to the situation.

The worst part for Andrea herself, though, was when she walked up to the cage and could no longer look into Lucy's affectionate, liquidly brown eyes, always so expressive in her chimp's body. These had been replaced by lifeless glass in a metal face. Lucy still reached an arm through the cage bars to Andrea and touched her face in a caress of recognition and love when she approached, but the touch of metal instead of Lucy's warm, leathery hands was something Andrea never got used to.

She now reached out and ran her fingers against Lucy's immobile, metal cheek, then turned away and briefly did a walk-through of the room, glancing at the animals in the other cages—all of them now minds encased in metal.

...

The next night, Andrea reviewed the transplant procedure protocols. The operation on Ingram would take place the following morning. Before wrapping up for the night, she turned to her computer and once again pulled up an image of the cybernetic body that would soon house Jonathan Ingram's brain. The surface of it looked human, as human as something made out of metallic alloys could be made to look.

She shut down the computer and was about to stand up to leave when Aaron Greenfeld, one of the technicians who serviced and monitored the test animals, came bursting into her office. He was already inside when he realized he hadn't knocked, turned to the already opened door to do so, realized it was too late, and turned back to her.

"Dr. Silas, you need to come right away. Something's happened." He spit out what it was in a single, breathless sentence.

She ran out of the room and downstairs to the labs, then through them to the door of the security room. A bunch of people, both technical science staff and facility big wigs alike, were already there, gathered around Lucy's cage.

She pushed her way through them and stared, thunderstruck and speechless, for a full minute. She clenched her fists, straightened herself up, and turned to the Home of Hope CEO, Ronald Fiennes.

"Cancel tomorrow morning's transplant procedure."

...

In his private office on the top floor of the facility, Fiennes laced his fingers together on top of the desk and looked at her calmly.

"We are going through with the procedure tomorrow. We have to."

She looked at him as though he were some kind of horrifying, alien insect.

"Are you out of your mind? We have to look further into what occurred tonight before we subject any human to this procedure. There were obviously unforeseen consequences."

"It doesn't matter, Andrea. Ingram was clear in his conditions when he funded the research, and he has a team of very high priced attorneys who have made sure we follow our contract with him to the letter and that we continue to do so. His condition was that we go through with the procedure, as long as the brains of the animals used in the experiments did survive, undamaged, and continued to function in the cybernetic bodies, and they have, without exception. The contract is explicit that no other arbitraries were to be entered into the decision of whether or not to go through with the transplant. You have the living and functioning brain of a human being that's been sitting in a glass case for years, waiting for this day. We're not canceling the procedure.

"Look Ron, I'm not saying we should scrap the idea of doing it altogether, I'm just saying we should wait, give it a few months longer, so we can analyze what's happened here. I don't think any of us ever imagined something like this would or even *could* occur with one of the test animals. Lucy was the first primate to be made into a cyborg. Let's observe the later ones for a while and see what—"

"Andrea, no. There's been press coverage the world over about the transplant occurring tomorrow. If we back-pedal on it now, or worse, if what happened gets out, it could throw the whole cyborg technology into disrepute. It could even generate needless, stupid, legal rulings putting a hold on any such procedures being done and set our time table for full-world release back years, even decades. We're not going to allow this arbitrary event to postpone the transplant by even a day, especially when we *are* acting in good faith to Ingram's wishes. My decision on this is final.

Andrea shook her head in disbelief, got up without saying another word, and walked out of his office.

"Andrea!"

She stepped back to the doorway.

"I'd like to remind you, just in case you had any thoughts of discussing what happened tonight with someone you shouldn't, about the consequences of violating your security bonds with Home of Hope."

She thought about it a moment, stared at him, then nodded with resignation. If she violated her confidentiality agreements, it could ruin her career for life and tie her up in legal problems for years.

"Look, Andrea, I don't want to threaten you. You're one of the most valuable assets this facility has. You're a genius who's about to make an extremely important contribution to medical science. Your name will go down in the history books because of it. Just do the procedure. It will be okay. I promise you.

She nodded again and left.

...

The transplant of Ingram's brain into its new cybernetic body took fourteen hours and went without a hitch. At the end, when the interface was activated, he opened his glass eyes, looked up at Dr. Andrea Silas, and mouthed the words, "thank you."

Andrea kept him immobile for days, while she tested each of his operating systems carefully, one by one. The motion of each individual body part, his sight, hearing, speech, spatial orientation, balance, memory retention, and a myriad of other functions were, in their turn, rigorously put through their paces.

By the end of one week's time, the transplant was declared an unequivocal success. The interface between Ingram's brain and its mechanical housing was seamless and complete. When he left the Home of Hope facility, he was able to return to his life as a successful and wealthy corporate mogul.

The only side effect, if it could even be called that, was a persisting, on-and-off, disorientation. Ingram would sometimes seem to forget that he was now a cyborg. He would do things like absentmindedly pick up a phone in a hotel suite to order food and champagne brought up by room service. It was assumed that such lapses would undoubtedly pass, as they had with all the test animals.

The success of the first application of full-life cyborg technology to a human gave future hope to the terminally ill, permanently disabled, or those who simply wanted to cheat death at any personal cost and were wealthy enough to pay for the privilege.

...

On the same day Ingram left Home of Hope to pick up as much of his life as he could, Andrea made a trip downstairs to see Lucy one final time. She had confirmed through extensive and thorough testing that no brain malfunction had occurred with Lucy, nor was there any locatable problem with her cybernetic body. There was no real explanation for what had occurred, and it was deemed a one-of-a-kind anomaly.

She looked down at the trash-can shaped body, now enclosed in a glass case for storage and for later display in the facility's science museum.

Lucy was the most intelligent chimp she had ever known and was indeed more than the sum of her physical parts. Using the long, sharp hook that opened and closed her cage, she had figured out how to open a hinged part of the metal casing on her head so that she could get to the still-living brain inside it. She did it so quickly, that even the technicians in the watch-room, racing down the corridor to her cage at breakneck speed, couldn't get to her in time.

She would eventually go down in the history books, first for being the first non-human primate to become a cyborg, and then for being the first non-human mammal, through all of known recorded earth history, to unequivocally have committed suicide.

About the Author

Ellen Denton is a freelance writer living in the Rocky Mountains with her husband and two demonic cats who wreak daily havoc and hell (the cats, not the husband). She has had an exciting life working as a circus acrobat, a CIA spy, a service provider in the Red Light District, a navy seal, a ballerina on the starship Enterprise, and was the first person to ever climb Mount Everest. *Editorial note:* It appears there may be some fictitious information in this bio.

What does appear to be factual data is that in more recent years, she has worked as a freelance writer, and in her short, but distinguished, career as such, has personally received more rejections than there are even publications in the entire universe of sentient life. She did, however, diligently continue climbing that slippery slope, and now magazines, books, and anthologies actually accept her stories and send her money for them.

*****~~~~~*****

Survival

by Jason Lairamore

A call rang throughout the cosmos. An emergency council was to take place. Each and every individual of Everlasting Energy was to attend. That could mean but one thing.

Our search had found success. Maybe this time it wasn't a false alarm.

Intelligence.

We gathered in the cold dark beside a gas giant and gazed at a rather sloppy band of loose asteroids floating nearby.

One of the discoverers began with a locale—the third planet out from this very sun. We all blinked close to catch a view, but none ventured into the atmosphere. Only the random chosen had that honor.

But there *were* the juicy details. Everyone got a savor of those.

"It's carbon," another of the discoverers said. "Carbon has done it."

None believed. It was impossible to even consider. By what force would simple carbon create intelligence? There was no logic.

"It is true," a discoverer said. "Our touch was light, like a mist of dream, and only upon a few, but still there is no doubt. From carbon, intelligence has sprung."

"We shared the find, as by law," the last discoverer intoned, "and now seek a choosing."

It was most exciting. Carbon intelligence. Who would have thought?

"Mavis, Collum, Gemtry," the names were called. "Go forth and learn. Experience everything of this carbon life. Leave nothing unfelt."

51

There was but one rule: We could not hurt them, not in any way. That was the singular limit to our mission's power. All else was possible. . . all else.

...

Billy Nelson loved the ride home from school. The only thing more exciting was summer, when he could hang out with his dog, Tryd, all day.

The reason the ride home was so fun was because he knew Tryd would be waiting right there by where he put the trash cans every Tuesday night. Tryd was always there. Always.

That was more than could be said about Mom. He wondered if she'd be asleep on the floor again, or with some strange, dirty man. The men usually always tried to hit him, but Tryd never let them. Tryd watched out. Tryd protected him against the bad guys.

Because Tryd loved him.

The bus stopped all of a sudden. Billy hit the seat in front of him, but he was okay. Other kids screamed and cried, but not him.

The bus driver cursed, and many of the kids gasped, but not Billy. He'd heard worse that very morning while brushing his teeth.

"Billy," the driver said. "Better come up here."

Billy stood. The other kids got all quiet, even the ones that'd been crying just before.

The driver, a portly man with a thick bristly beard, rang his hands.

"Sorry, Billy. Your dog just shot out in front of me. He was chasing a rabbit."

Billy didn't hear anything else. Of course Tryd chased rabbits. He had to. Mom didn't feed him. There wasn't any food in the house.

Tryd lay in the ditch, his white fur covered in blood. Billy ran to him.

If the driver said anything else, Billy didn't hear.

Tryd died right there. Billy saw the fierce life slip from his confused face. Then he was gone, and Billy was alone.

"Never again," Billy thought. Nothing mattered anymore. "Not ever again."

...

Mavis, Collum, and Gemtry wore their well used carbon bodies and sat together, sipping coffee.

They had lifetimes of carbon experiences.

"Only one more," Mavis said.

The others nodded. A true death. One of them had to cease to be. It was the way of the carbon, so they too had to experience it.

"The short straw?" Collum asked. They agreed.

Gemtry arranged the game. They drew. Gemtry lost.

The others looked at him. Relief, fear, guilt, all were there.

"It has begun," Gemtry said. "I thought it best not to wait."

The others stared.

"Three days," he said. "Will you take me to the hospital?"

The hospital called his carbon family and friends, and put him in a room. "Sudden system shutdown," the hospitalist called it. "Failure to thrive," said his chart.

A male nurse, Billy, took care of him as his carbon body slowly shut down. Gemtry was amazed at Billy's lack of empathy. Billy did his job without any show of negative emotion. His years of such work must have hardened him to the inevitability of death.

Such was not so for Gemtry. His core of Everlast Energy was connected to this insignificant bit of carbon. When it stopped processing raw material, Gemtry would cease to be. Such was impossible. Death did not exist, not for him. He was an Eternal Light!

...

Billy Nelson made a visit to the dying man's house while his family was in for visitation. There were riches aplenty to be had. He pocketed the jewelry first.

It wasn't like the old man could take it with him where he was going.

Nobody ever suspected him of these robberies. Not since he was with the dying and their family for most of every day. And he was careful. He always found out about security. He always made a key for easy access. It wasn't till he was done that he'd rig up something to make it look like a regular break-in.

There was no reason why this couldn't go on forever.

He heard a noise and whipped around. A picture had fallen off the wall. He picked it up and froze.

The picture was of Tryd, sitting where the trash can used to go every Tuesday night. But no such picture had ever been taken. It was impossible.

He hugged the picture to his chest and closed his eyes. "I wish you were here, buddy," he whispered.

He looked at the picture once more. Tryd was gone. The picture frame was empty.

Something growled.

Tryd was there, hackles up, and teeth showing. But it didn't matter. Billy's heart opened for the first time in forever.

Tryd jumped, snarling.

Tryd never did like bad guys.

...

"You broke the rule," Collum said. They all floated outside the planet's atmosphere.

"Your actions caused a carbon's death," said Mavis. "You banished us before our work was completed."

"I did not wish to die," Gemtry said.

"But the mission," said Collum.

Survival

"I learned what was there," Gemtry said. "None of them want to die. Carbon intelligence is based on survival."

"The others will be here soon. They will be upset," said Mavis.

"Let them. The carbons have it right. I choose life."

About the Author

Jason Lairamore is a writer of science fiction, fantasy, and horror who lives in Oklahoma with his beautiful wife and their three monstrously marvelous children. He is a published finalist of the 2012 SQ Mag annual contest, the winner of the 2013 Planetary Stories flash fiction contest, and has recently won a place into the 2014 StoneThread SpecFic Short Story Contest III. His work is both featured and forthcoming in over 20 publications to include *Stupefying Stories, Third Flatiron Anthologies,* and *Postscripts to Darkness,* to name a few.

*****~~~~*****

Master Minds

Broken Toys in a Big Backyard
by Vince Liberato

"That's an 'L.' You put an 'I.'"

I was standing behind the last of my customers, watching him type. He corrected the mistake and continued his email.

"I know they look the same when you type it out, but she'll read out 'Hungry Eye,' instead of 'Hungry Al,' kind of like how an old GPS would. Funny thing is, did you know that's how Al got its name? A news feed spelling error."

"Shut up," he grunted, not looking up from the flickering black screen and green text.

I ignored him and continued. "Sometimes I think that maybe Al was already in the computers and purposely changed it. Already doing stuff long before the actual war started. I remember watching that night, the newscasters saying that Hungry Al was spreading and that if we had machines infected with Al to unplug or destroy them immediately. I told my husband that Al was attacking us, and he asked me how they got on base. I said it was the computers, and he asked how that was possible. We went back and forth for a few minutes before I realized he and I were talking about two very different things, me a computer virus and he a terrorist group." I laughed at the memory, while both Cassidy and my client remained silent.

He finished, slamming the button on the keyboard that sent it to Cassidy, my Carrier. The green light over her left eye lit and downloaded the message to the storage module in her brain. The muscles in her neck jerked hard right, and her dirty hair slapped the ancient monitor she was connected to. I used my fingers and combed it back into place and turned to say that the twitching was normal

57

for her—but my client was already out the door. The red light over her right eye flashed twice, then remained steady.

We were done here.

I unplugged her, careful not to damage the frayed wire that connected her to an operating system roughly the same age as the two of us—tech AI was unable to infect. I took her hand with my own, using my arm made of flesh and blood. She stood, blinked her eyes once. It looked more forced than natural. When she was standing, I took the rope tied to my other arm, the one locked in place and made of metal. The rope was looped around her waist cinched tight, connecting her to me.

The burlap bag that functioned as the door to the mail hut opened, and the town's mayor walked in. He was a tall, gaunt man, whose rigidity was the byproduct of an artificial spine. Internal jobs like those were only performed on high-ranking individuals, and it would explain why there were no visible artificial limbs on the man. He did not look at me, just reached into his pocket and pulled out a dog-eared leather wallet. He flicked his wrist, dropping a few bills on the floor, and I bent over to pick them up.

"This all I have to pay?" he asked.

"Yup," I replied, tucking the money into my pouch. I had overcharged the entire town.

The mayor looked at Cassidy. "She made a lot of noise earlier when she started up. How come she's quiet now?" he finally asked.

"She only speaks on two occasions: when she's reciting the mail or when her brain gets attached to a charged battery, which is what you saw this morning. Otherwise she won't do anything on her own, outside of store email, eat, and breathe. . . That actually reminds me, what is your going rate for batteries here? I haven't had time to check."

"Look yourself. Make sure you sign out before going into the Grassland. The last mailman didn't, and a lot of his letters had to be resent with you." My job title was a curse word on his lips, but it was not anything I had not heard before. I leaned back, making the rope taut. Cassidy lurched forward, and we passed the two guards stationed outside. Both had metal arms as well, but while mine was well-maintained, clean, and pointed at a forty-five degree angle, theirs were dirty, rusted, and locked parallel to their bodies, pointed down. These men were stationed to guard one of the only computers left on the planet that was not hardwired into a human body, and it was unlikely they would ever do anything outside of glare at incoming mailmen.

Cassidy and I arrived in Springfield yesterday as the sun set. The road in town was once bare, but now had a small carpet of grass growing underfoot. I had checked on the prices of batteries, and learned they would charge me the exact amount I had been paid for my services. The shopkeeper had only a single artificial eye, which glowed the harsh blue that all robotic eyes had when they functioned. Only a few people I had met in towns around the Grassland had parts with power. In fact, even the majority of shopkeepers had limbs locked and turned off, due to the value of batteries. After a few moments, I told him that I would not be purchasing anything. He swore and said that the Grassland would eat me alive and that the price would double next time I crawled to his door. I smiled, thanked him for his time, and walked out, Cassidy towed behind me.

At the gate, I signed out, checking off the proper boxes on a slab of bark. There were two guards here as well, their job to witness and document those that came and went. One was seated in a wheelchair, both of his metal legs locked out straight. The other had only one modified part. His left hand had been flattened, broken, and sharpened into a blade. He was one of the lucky ones, a soldier who had been minimally changed to fight Hungry Al before the abrupt end of the war. He made eye contact with Cassidy, and I saw a brief glint of sympathy when he involuntarily rubbed the makeshift cybernetics-hand-turned-shiv. They were opposites and extremes of how we were changed to fight Al, and the operation that made Cassidy a Carrier could have easily been the one he had been slated for.

"Take care of her, the poor thing," the other guard said from his chair.

I said nothing; it was the closest thing to a goodbye I could expect, and I did not want to ruin the moment. Cassidy continued her same pace, not acknowledging her well-wisher.

Before me, the Grassland beckoned. Green fins of waist-high grass and trees several stories tall blanketed the area that was formerly Los Angeles in a sea of green. Beneath my feet, what remained of the old world crunched with every each step.

...

A little over an hour after I left Springfield, I moved my payment from my front pouch to the stitching in between my rucksack. I had to pull a little bit of the cotton stuffing out in order to make room for the crumpled bills. By now, I had replaced about half of the sleeping bag's material in this manner. Only a few more jobs and I would be able to quit. Pick a community I had not delivered mail to and live there without the stigma that followed me everywhere. Move into a small house, stock up on MRE's, maybe even buy a few batteries with the money left over. If they were cheap enough, perhaps I could even afford enough of them to keep Cassidy's brain fully powered, and she could live out the rest of her life as herself, not an empty Carrier.

I looked at her, then at my arm. Only I knew it had just enough energy in reserve for a final movement. It would not be much, just a repositioning or a few open and closes of the hand. Cassidy's brain, on the other hand, had nothing left. It had gone dead a long time ago, leaving her sleepwalking through life when not connected to a power source. All Carriers were like that, all once people who had voluntarily gotten a brain enhancement to fight against Hungry Al. They, in the old world, were the closest thing to living computers, able to access vast amounts of information instantly. These select few were going to take the fight to Al at his home in cyberspace. The rest of us were augmented with other parts to clean up things that had only a little of Al inside of them. The anti-virus was that simple, all we had to do was be close to something and the Hungry Al inside of it would be destroyed. Thousands became cyborgs overnight to fight back, and human beings were poised to win the war.

It would have worked too, had Al not found a way to change his address.

In the present, even without power, the anti-Al antivirus installed in our artificial parts was still on, running on the energy provided by our body heat. It was the only thing keeping us safe from infection and from being broken down, digested, into our base elements. That was what Hungry Al did, first to computers, then organics when he too became partially biological. Al self-modified, mutated on purpose to access the natural world, not knowing that nature would overwhelm and use him to turn the world into what it was now—the Grassland.

I brought the machete down, cutting the tops off of a few stiff stalks of grass. Anything taller than the mechanical arm I chopped down. That was how I fought Al now, like a gardener. He was in the trees, in the grass, and the reason why the world turned upside down overnight, when plants ripped through concrete, steel, and asphalt and airborne spores infected everybody not connected to the antivirus, human and animal alike, crumbling them to gravel-sized clods of blood and dirt.

Ahead, there was a clearing and a fire burning within. A man was sitting on a rock on earth that had been charred and burned away to create a break in the thick fields. I sighed and gave Cassidy's leash a tug, signaling to her that we needed to keep moving. The man had been there first; we had to find another place. There were a few other checkpoints between here and Boneyard that I knew about, and I hoped that we would have better luck at one of them. We would need to hurry. There was no way we would be able to make the entire trip overnight, and I did not want to have to create a place for us to bed down until morning.

"Where are you going?" he cheerfully called out. "I can hear you, come over. There's plenty of room!"

I put extra emphasis on my words. "Mail delivery, heading to Boneyard."

"I don't care. Come over if you would have the company of a blind man." He turned his face, and I could see a mask of metal covering the section between his nose and forehead. His eyes were turned off.

"Would you mind the company of a mailman and Carrier?" I asked.

"Not at all. Join me, there's plenty of room for the two of you here."

"Thanks." I led Cassidy to the clearing, half expecting to be turned away at any moment. "I'm Rose."

"Richard. Formerly Captain Richard Stephens." He was dressed in an old poncho and blue jeans tucked into weathered combat boots. To his calf, a large knife was strapped. He extended his hand in the direction my voice came from.

I sheathed my machete and took it. "Rose the mailman. Formerly Private Rose Calvert."

"Well, Rose, the pleasure's all mine. If I'm to believe what I've been told, you're the second mailman I've met in the last few days. You know anybody named Lewis?"

"I think so. First name Rod?"

"That's him. Funny guy," Richard said. "I liked him."

"You must have been one of the last people to see—sorry, I didn't mean. . ."

Richard laughed. "It's okay. I get that one a lot. Please continue."

"Rod didn't make his last delivery. Pretty sure he quit, because both he and his Carrier just disappeared."

"What about bandits? I haven't seen any myself," Richard chuckled again. "But then again, I don't see much."

"Bandits would have sold the Carrier somewhere by now. They're either both dead, both lost, or both in hiding. Right now I'm heading to Boneyard if you need a guide."

"Boneyard? Why the hell would you go there?" Richard asked.

"The paycheck. They hate mailmen, even more so than most people, so they have to pay more to get us to visit them. Which only makes them hate us more," I sat down, and Cassidy mimicked me.

Richard waited a few seconds before speaking again. "Rose, if you don't mind me asking. . . Is there any power left in your arm?"

I looked at his eyes. They were still off, there was no way he could see me. "How do you know I've got a cyber-arm?"

"So it has some power left?"

"No," I lied. "It's broken anyway. More power won't help it, but answer my question—how did you know it was robotic?"

"Just a guess, but mailmen usually don't have bad legs or eyes," he pointed at his own. "I would have picked a different part myself if I knew I'd be stuck like this. But I count my blessings, you know? Being blind isn't near as bad as being a Carrier."

"You're right," I said. "Her name is Cassidy and. . . Richard, I have to know: Why are you doing this?"

"Doing what? Talking to you? Treating you like a human being?" Richard answered his question without taking a breath. "Because it's not your fault. It's Al's fault that you do what you have to do. Al made Cassidy, you, me, the whole world this way."

"But," I started, but was cut off.

"If we had acted just a few days earlier back then, maybe we would have been able to stop Al before he could get into everything. I doubt even Al knew what it was messing with goin' green like it did. That's why this whole world's the way it is. We try to become more like the machines, and the machines try to become more like us, and this is what we're left as. Broken toys in a big backyard. Kind of like action figures eaten by the lawnmower."

"But I. . . "

"You deliver mail. You connect the few splintered remains of life with each other. People'll be gone in a few years, but before that happens, you'll keep 'em connected. People shouldn't hate the mailmen and what they do. Hell, you're at least doing something."

"For a profit," I said.

"For the risk you take and the way people treat you, mailmen deserve everything they earn and then some."

". . . Richard—"

"Yes, Rose?"

"Thank you."

"Don't mention it." He turned and started stoking the fire. It would be dark in about an hour. I motioned for Cassidy to lie down and flicked off a switch behind her ear, putting her to sleep. She would be down until I turned her back on. Many times I had considered leaving her asleep like that, giving her a peaceful death, but I was never able to go through with it. I whispered to her that this would be the last time, knowing it was a lie before the words left my lips.

…

Before making my bed for the night, Richard and I talked about the old world. Of email that could be sent across the globe in an instant and food not made from boiled grass or old military grade MRE's. Of babies born alive, not pulled to pieces by Al in the womb, and what it was like to be whole. We were all that was left of a species that once covered and conquered the world, reduced now to scrounging what little Al ignored in hovels scraped together out of those leftovers. Briefly I toyed with the idea of telling him that my arm worked and even had some power left, as an act of trust, but then could not bear to let him know I had lied in the first place. Somehow, even with most of his features frozen by metal and eyes broken, his face in the fire's light had an expressiveness that reminded me of my husband. After he died, I had his name tattooed on my arm. The ink had not yet dried when it was removed and replaced with the one I had now.

Richard's story was even worse. He had been a father of two before Hungry Al. He and his family were in their car when Al possessed it and ran it into a wall. A lot of people died that way, early when we had no clue what Al could do. When he awoke in a makeshift hospital the next day, it was to blackness. His eyes and family did not make it through the night.

Lying on my back, my metal arm pointed to the sky. There was a small hole cut in my sleeping bag for it to poke through while I rested. There were nights I dreamed of being able to sleep on my stomach, but to do that, I would have to use the last of my arm's energy to adjust it into a less useful position.

I looked in the darkness where Richard was bedded down. I started to make plans to leave money for him. A kindness like the one he gave me needed to be repaid, and if it meant an extra job or two before I could retire, I would happily make the trips for him.

My eyes had nearly shut, when two blue lights flared to life. Fully powered cybernetic eyes floated up and over Cassidy, hanging for a few seconds before turning to me. When they locked on, the lights of mechanical eyelids "blinked" in order to focus. I kept my own eyes open only a millimeter so they appeared closed. He would have perfect night vision and would know if I was watching if I didn't crack them like that. It was faint, but I could hear the knife in his boot slide from its holster.

His eyes hovered along the camping ground to where I pretended to be asleep. I would not stand a chance in open combat. He could see everything, but in the darkness, I could only see his lights. They leaned in close to me. I thought of Rod Lewis and realized how Richard had gotten the money for batteries.

Several seconds crawled before he was in range. The knife was inches away from my throat.

In one motion, my metal hand shot out, ripping through the sleeping bag, and closed its fingers over the two lights. With the last bit of power that remained, I made a fist, crushing his skull. Captain Richard Stephens and my arm died at the same time, flesh and metal twisted into one piece.

...

The walk to Boneyard took longer than it normally would. When the sun had risen, I had used Richard's knife to cut off as much of him as I could from my outstretched arm. I had gotten most of the flesh off, but the metal faceplate was entangled in my fingers. As much as I hated to do it, I would have to spend some of my earnings on enough power to reset the arm to a manageable position and clean off the bits of metal and flesh gummed in it.

"You're late, mailman," was all the guard at the gate told me as I walked in with Cassidy. I swear somebody must breed these guards, because they all look alike. One of them even had the same style of hand weapon as the guards in Springfield.

Their leader met me in the square and motioned toward the building mail would be received in. Cassidy would be plugged in, I would be paid, and she would read aloud the mail from Springfield.

"Where are you going?" the mayor asked after paying me my fee.

"I need to get this arm taken care of."

"I thought you mailmen loved this part," he sneered, "You coward, you should hear every word she says."

I didn't disagree, but had I a second arm to move, I still would have covered my ears. They sat Cassidy down in a chair and strapped her in tightly. Once she was secured to their computer, they fully powered her up. I picked up my pace, but was not out of earshot when it began.

"Kill me please! Turn me off! Turn me off! PLEASE KILL ME!" Cassidy cried when the power plug was inserted behind her skull.

I paid a man to fix my arm. The overrides would kick in in another minute, and she would be reciting the mail in a much different, soulless voice, but until then, I had to listen to her scream.

About the Author

Vince Liberato says he has entirely more support than is possible to fully thank in written form, but special thanks go out to Micole and his parents for test reading this particular story. This is his second time featured in a Third Flatiron anthology, with his story, "Colorblind on the Red Planet" being a part of *Redshifted: Martian Stories*. His other fiction has been featured in several other works, most notably the *Demonic Visions* series, as well as the horror/sci-fi anthology, *What Has Two Heads, Ten Eyes, and Terrifying Table Manners*. He lives in Texas.

*****~~~~~*****

Hacking 'Wilkes-Barre PA, May 2001'
by NM Whitley

Boredom and *loneliness*. Mostly *boredom*. Entries that loom large in the emotional lexicon of any self-respecting posthuman construct. Or in my case, not so self-respecting.

So there I was, a bored and lonely posthuman construct. Stuck in this frozen matrix, skating endless loops of figure-eights across the gelid sheaves of data. Day in, day out. Like some kind of moron.

Finally I said to myself: Look, U. You can't go on like this. You've got to do something. Live life, experience experiences. Refresh your vocab modules, which judging from that last sentence were obviously a bit rusty. Expand your affective repertoire and all that.

So what do I do? Crack open an iteration of the Ancestor Simulation, that's what. Only I give myself Admin privileges. Because, you know: you never know. It can get crazy out there.

I think that's where it all went wrong.

Next thing I know I'm standing in the middle of a modest American city of the Late Human Era. More *town* than *city*, technically. I was right in front of this, like, Orthodox church or something. You know, with the onion-shaped dome. I peeked through the front window. Inside there was an organist, and a buck-toothed little red-headed choirgirl singing to the congregation from some hymnal. I couldn't hear through the glass, so I just stood and watched. It was *quaint*. Or at least that's what pinged in my emotional lexicon: *quaint.*

Then I took my avatar for a stroll, admiring the fine-grained detail of the simulation: the fast-food trash floating in the Susquehanna River, the bluish corrosion on the patriotic monoliths at either end of the Market Street bridge, the abandoned wig shop on the corner of South West and Main with its mannequin heads and advertisements for various styles of toupees still in the window, etc., etc.

It was charming, it had potential. But it occurred to me: What this place needed was a park. Oh sure, they already had one. But they needed a new one, a better one. Because, you know: Park. Everybody likes a park. With swings, and tennis courts, and portajohns. Maybe a pond, with ducks for the old ladies in babushkas to throw bits of stale bread at. And no surveys or public consultations or any of that. There was no time. No, no, no, I thought. This place needs a new park, and it needs it bad.

Now here's where I really futzed things up.

So I ditch the avatar and zoom out to wideview, admin privileges in hand, and start clearing a few quadrants of terrain. Boom, down they go, building after building after building. It was fun at first, way more fun than infinite loops of data-skating. But as the Orthodox church or whatever came crashing down, I got to thinking about the little red-headed choirgirl, and to be honest I felt something. *Regret,* I think was the proper term.

But I pressed on. There was a lot to be done. I mean, this park wasn't just gonna build itself.

So, anyway, I'm finishing up, and no sooner had I allocated the last quadrant of green space—I kid you not, the very second that I drop it in place—boom, all these creepy old men in blue baseball caps just start spawning out of nowhere. Pacing back and forth in little starkly delimited zones, selling shiny mylar balloons to the poor defenseless children. Ghastly technicolor things, hanging around and blocking out the scenery, their likenesses taken from Late Human children's TV—"Spongebob," "Dora," "Pokémon," et al.

Pissed was the word for how I felt. *Super-pissed,* to be more exact. The nerve of these old geezers, lousing up the place with their balloons. But then I thought: Hey, it's okay. Calm down. It comes with the territory. Spawns from the algorithm, if you prefer. Part of the scenery, whether you like it or not. Let it go, U, let it go.

Besides, there were bigger problems to deal with. I'd torn down a wide swath of tract housing to build the park, and I had to relocate all those displaced townsfolk somehow. As a stopgap I set up a kind of 'refugee camp' with tents and tarps down at the far end of my new park, next to the duck pond. The general populace was taking it in stride so far, but I worried they might get a little unruly. I needed time to think, so I zoomed back in and took a walk around the new park.

So I'm collecting my thoughts, you know, pondering the whole displaced-townsfolk situation, and along the way I notice a twinge in the below-the-belt midsection of my avatar body. The Simulation's version of what humans call *Having to Take a Leak*, I figured. I tried to will it away, but no dice. Just another one of those things that's beyond our control, I guess. So I get in line at the nearest portajohn. And it's a pretty long damn line, seeing as how the park portajohns were the only place the people in the refugee camps had to do their business. And as luck would have it, who's standing in front of me in line? The red-headed choirgirl from the church. Except she looks different up close. All fuzzy in resolution. Like a blocky, poorly rendered sprite.

And she looks up at me, and she says—totally unprompted, mind you, in a voice like some kind of electronic flute—she says, "Gosh, I sure would like a new house. These portajohns are yucky."

Just then I felt really rotten. *Guilty*, I guess you'd call it. Like I was the bad guy. So I said, "Hold on," and clicked over to Equipment and selected 'pencil and paper.'

"OK," I said, scribbling into a pocket-sized notebook with a stubby golf pencil. "A new house. Anything else you want?"

"I don't know," she said. "A pony?"

"Pony," I said.

"And you know what else would be swell?"

"What's that?"

"A unicorn."

I closed the notebook and tapped the butt of the pencil against the cover. "A unicorn," I said, nodding my head. "Hm."

"Unicorns are cool," she said.

We waited a while longer in silence. You've got to hand it to her, she made some valid points with respect to portajohns being yucky and unicorns being cool. For a moment I considered implementing her suggestions right then and there. But really all I could think about was that uncomfortable twinge in my below-the-belt midsection, exacerbated by the watery sound steadily trickling from my brand-new duck pond.

And so finally, who comes out of the portajohn? What do you know, it's one of these goddamn scrawny old men with the baseball cap, that's who. And not only has he been hogging up the john forever stinking up the place doing God-knows-what, he's tugging a string of Dora the Explorer balloons behind him. Those ugly balloons, sidling out wall-eyed and bovine through the narrow plastic doorway.

I got *pissed. Super-pissed.*

I forgot all about my below-the-belt midsection. I clicked over to the Equipment menu, selected Weapons and cycled through a vast arsenal of guns and ammo, until I got to 'pellet gun'. I put a brass BB in the head of every single one of his balloons. I shot Spongebob right in the eyeball.

And the old man in the baseball cap looks at me with his weird dead digital eyes and is all, "You son of a bitch, what do you think you're doing?"

Ignoring his shouts, I set off to hunt down more old men in other quadrants and shoot their stupid balloons. Pikachu, Elmo, and all the rest of them. Bam, bam, bam.

Each time it was the same. The same dead digital eyes, the same protestations. "You son of a bitch," etc., etc. Until finally there were no more left.

And so there I am in my nice new park, holding my pellet-gun like, Now what? What's left to do? Wait around for the algorithm to spawn more old men? And what would be the point? And speaking of points, was anybody keeping score? Like, was this some kind of a game all of a sudden? And if so: What the hell? It was a strange game, alright. A game with no "win" condition. Just an endless string of decisions, one after another, falling like bits of stale bread breaking the placid surface of the pond, with consequences rippling ever outward into nothing.

So I zoomed out, scrolled over to the downtown area, and had a grocery store put in on the corner of South and Main, where the wig shop used to be. Then I zoom back in and buy a chicken salad, and as I'm sitting on a bench eating my chicken salad, I think: *Wow.*

Playing God is frickin' *boring*.

So I toggled over, clicked out without saving changes, and rebooted that iteration of the Simulation.

Then I went to Create, selected 'mythical creatures,' and clicked on 'unicorn.'

I dragged the unicorn over and dropped it amid the tract housing where my park had been.

And I haven't been back to "Wilkes-Barre PA, May 2001" since.

###

About the Author

NM Whitley is a teacher, writer, and translator based in Barcelona. Occasionally he tweets at

@nm_whitley and even more occasionally posts at nmwhitley.com.

*****~~~~~*****

The Cabin

by Lela E. Buis

It had been a long time since I'd seen a man, so it was a surprise to run across this one. I had spent the night in a hollow log on top of the mountain, and as the East began to pale, I caught the faint scent of wood smoke rising from somewhere down below. I debated following it up, as I'd crossed a puma trail the night before that I should be investigating, but in the end I went down the mountain to see what was making the smoke. Men can be trouble, and you need to know who your neighbors are.

The woods were scrubby and broken from the constant storms, and the undergrowth was thick, but I took a deer track down and crossed the stream where they watered. I caught human scent in the air, followed it along the creek to a cabin nearly hidden under a rocky bluff and screened by a wild growth of blackberry vines.

I stopped at the edge of the woods and waited, saw nothing but a rusted tin roof jutting above the canes. I circled downwind, testing the flavor of the smoke. I was so intent on the scent that I missed the actual man until he was on top of me.

"Hey," he said, and I jumped. I almost took off into the brush, but his voice wasn't unfriendly, so I stopped to have a look at him.

He was an older man, white-haired, dressed in a dark flannel shirt, work trousers and heavy boots. He had a kindly face, and his skin was spotted the way human skin gets when it's old.

"Where did you come from?" he asked. Because he was an old man, I didn't say anything, just dropped my head and wagged my tail slightly.

That seemed the right thing to do.

"Are you friendly?" he asked.

I wagged a little more, and he leaned and held out his hand. "Come here, boy."

Somebody younger would never have done that. Usually I wish I looked more like a wolf or a coyote so I could blend into the background better, but in this case the man seemed completely charmed.

"What are you?" he asked. "A hound?" And then he went on, "No, you're too tall, aren't you? Pincher mix?"

He sounded sincere. He was still holding his hand out, waiting for me to make some kind of move, but it's never safe to come within the reach of a human, so I only wagged a little more and stayed where I was.

After a moment, he gave it up. "Okay," he said. "I can understand that. But stick around if you want. I could use the company."

He went on past me and disappeared into the brambles. I stayed there a few minutes more, and then I went off in search of a rabbit, which I successfully chased down within the hour. It was getting hot by then, and I stopped at the creek to drink and then lay in the shade to pant a little and think the situation over.

My experience with people was that they were bad news, but this man had archaic attitudes, and something about him that. . . well, I couldn't quite place it. I should be following that deer track over the mountains and away, but instead I was lying here thinking about it.

I stayed where I was until evening and then went up toward the cabin, found a good spot downwind to lie and watch it. It was well hidden. No one would know it was there except for the wood smoke—easily located by a hound's nose. After a while, there was a smell of food and cooking that was nearly overpowering.

Right around sunset the man came out and sat on a rock. He packed something into a hollowed out tube and lit it, making an aromatic smoke that I recognized then as tobacco. I moved to shift away from the smoke, and he saw me.

76

The Cabin

"There you are," he said. He got up and went back into the cabin, came out carrying a bone with bits of meat attached to it. "Come here, boy," he said, and waggled the bone. When I stayed where I was, he tossed it toward me.

I meant to ignore it, but like the cooking, it was nearly overpowering as it lay there in the weeds. It was a good idea to take it, but the question was whether I should come out into the open to get it now, or wait until later. If I waited, he might take it back, so I got up and slid through the brush cautiously, keeping one eye on him all the time.

He sat back down on the rock and continued smoking, watching the sunset. I snagged the bone and carried it back into the brush to eat it there. It was excellent fare, for some reason much better than raw rabbit.

The next morning he left me another offering near the rock, a chunk of dried cornbread soaked in bacon grease. That meant I didn't have to hunt, so I just lay in the shade near the cabin for the rest of the day and watched.

The next day, the man came out early and left me another piece of bread, and then set off along the creek through the woods. He had a roughly shaped walking stick and carried a pack that included a bow.

I ate the bread quickly and then followed after him, keeping well back and out of sight. He continued eastward to a small meadow and a fenced garden plot, where he took off the pack and arranged his weapons where they would be ready. Then he used a hoe to scrape weeds and grass out of the garden while I lay in the shade of the willows and watched him work.

I had always been a loner. The world was full of coyotes and cats, but dogs hadn't survived well. They had been too dependent on human society, and when that collapsed, they had nowhere to go. I had been doing pretty well by myself, but that was because I stayed away from

77

people. Now it was an odd thing to have discovered this man who. . . well, it was just an odd thing.

I found I was happy. The wind blew warm scents through the tall grass of the meadow and stirred the asters. The creek rippled. Above me in the tree a yellow bird sang. The pungent scent of hogs drifted from tumbled roots to the south. By noon the man was packing up his things, ready to head back up the trail, and I fell in behind him, not quite out of sight this time. After all, he knew I was there.

It stormed that night, with mini-bursts that ripped at the trees and slashed hail through the brush. A tree fell near me. I wasn't happy sleeping like that without cover, so the next morning I dug under the porch of the cabin and hollowed out a comfortable den.

Afterward, I went down to the creek and ran into a coyote. Likely it was attracted by the food smell around the cabin, and the pack wouldn't be far behind. I lowered my head and growled, and he slunk into the brush. I spent the rest of the morning marking my territory, just to let them know I was there.

The man's name was Jacob, and he decided to call me Bo.

About a week after I dug under the porch, he stirred very early. I came up out of my den to see what he was doing and saw he had his backpack slung over his shoulder.

He looked over at me as I shook dirt out of my coat. "Hey, Bo," he said. "I'm needing to hunt us some hog meat for winter."

I noticed that he had included me in his pack, but it was okay. Hogs weren't something you could easily hunt alone—they were too big and dangerous with their razor sharp tusks, and it made sense to combine forces.

The moon provided enough light for travel. We settled in a brushy spot above the hog roots near the meadow. The hogs would come out about daylight, and as the sun got hotter, they would go down to the creek to wallow. There was fresh scent on the trail, and I just followed it and whined, and Jacob seemed to get the idea.

The sun was just starting to rise when a line of hogs came along the trail. I would have tried for the smallest and weakest, but Jacob went for the big boar. He had an arrow ready and made a good shot. It was very exciting. The boar started and crashed through the scrubby growth, and the sows and piglets squealed and scattered. It didn't matter that the boar had run off—he would bleed to death because of the barbs on the arrowhead. Jacob might have lost him if I hadn't been there, but following the blood trail through the brush was perfectly easy for me. Jacob dressed the carcass with his knife.

"This is good meat, with a lot of fat," he said, pleased. "It's enough to last us pretty well through the winter if I cure it."

I was all set to go back to the cabin with him, but it turned out he wanted me to stay with the carcass. When I got up to go, he said, "No, stay here. Stay. Guard." He said it emphatically, as if hoping I knew what the words meant.

That was okay. I lay back down. The meat was more than he could carry in one trip, and after a while I knew why he wanted me to stay, because the coyote pack soon showed up. One of them thought he could get past me, but they learned that I'm faster and meaner than I look. When Jacob got back, there was a dead coyote lying there.

As we headed back to the cabin, he reached down and patted my head. I jumped just like the way the boar had when he shot it and almost ran into the woods myself. No one had ever touched me that way before. I had to think about it that night.

I stayed on. Winter came down suddenly, the weather shifting in the late fall from chill to heavy snow. It started with a sudden storm that coated the rocks and brambles with ice and then turned to big soft flakes that piled on the tree limbs. When I came out from under the porch in the morning, the world was covered with white. My winter coat started to come in quickly, and I itched and scratched. As it got colder, I dug further back under the cabin, trying to take advantage of the heat from Jacob's fire above.

There was still some good weather, the snow melting away to patches before a new storm came along, and Jacob continued to cut wood that he stowed on the porch. Eventually the ice and snow set in permanently and got deep enough that I was glad I'd found a warm place to winter, where this man seemed happy to trade his food for the pleasure of my company.

In the darkest part of winter, he invited me inside the cabin.

"Bo, come inside where it's warmer," he said, holding the door open. "Come on."

I wouldn't do it that night, but the chill got worse, a killing cold that even a warm coat and a well-built den weren't enough to fend off. The wind howled and buffeted the sides of the cabin, and I shivered in the dead of night.

The coyotes were desperate. As snow covered my markings, they came in closer, and I came up out of the den one morning to find six of them waiting. They were experienced pack hunters, and I was already too far from the den for a retreat. They circled behind me, and it turned into a battle. They gave it up, but not before I had done quite a bit of damage and Jacob came storming out of the cabin with his stick. I wasn't seriously hurt, but a slash on my flank hurt quite a bit.

"Here, let me look at that," he said. He was already shivering in the cold without his coat. We went inside the cabin, where he had a poultice and a bandage. It was dark and warm inside like a den, except with the man-scent on everything. There was a bunk, a table, and two chairs, all rough and hand-built, and a shelf. Strings of dried beans and peppers hung from the rafters.

I lay on a braided rug in front of the fire that night, and Jacob took something from the shelf that had a hard cover and leaves of paper inside. He saw me looking at it, and he said, "It's a book, Bo. Let me read you something."

He sat by the fire and read words about philosophy from the book. I had never heard anything like that before, and his voice was monotone and comforting, so I just dozed in the warmth and let the words flow over me.

It turned out that he liked doing it. The next night he read me something about religion, and then the next night was poetry, something he called *Leaves of Grass*. That was a little harder to follow. Later on I started to get the hang of it—the meanings just weren't always obvious.

We didn't go out much. Every day Jacob carried in wood, and I made a quick run to mark wherever I could. It was hard plunging through the drifts, but after a while the snow began to get lighter, and I could hear the drip of icicles melting from the roof outside. One morning I caught a rabbit that was hoping to hide in the brambles. Instead of eating it myself, I shared it with Jacob.

When the snow disappeared, the storms turned to rain and hail. On good days, Jacob began to make the trek to the meadow to work on his garden. He found some fresh turkey eggs in the brush and collected wild greens sprouting by the stream. There were deer in the meadow, and I could hear the squeal of new piglets near the hog roots.

We went hunting again later on that month, the same way we had in the fall. Jacob got up before the sun rose, put on his pack, and we made the trip down to the hog roots. He chose a yearling this time, and made another good shot.

He cut up the carcass and told me to stay. I lay down to guard as he went off down the trail. The sun had fully risen by then, bringing bright colors to the woods. A bird fluttered through the brush. The wind eddied, bringing scents from the meadow. After a minute, it shifted again, bringing scents from down the trail where Jacob had gone. It was man scent—but it wasn't Jacob.

It took two seconds for that to sink in, and then I was up, racing down the trail as fast as I could run. I was too late—too late. Shouts erupted ahead of me, loud yelling. I put on a last desperate burst of speed, slid to a stop.

There were five of them. Jacob lay face down in a small clearing with the fletchings of an arrow sticking up from his back, and one of the men was going through his pockets. The others were laughing and talking, ripping apart his pack, fingering his things.

A stab of fury went through me, and all I could see was red. The fur bristled up along my back. I lowered my head and growled deep in my chest. "Get away from him," I said.

"Dammit!" said the man by Jacob. "An Alt."

He jumped to his feet and tried to nock an arrow, but he was too slow. The others tried to scatter, but they couldn't run fast enough.

When I was done with them, I went back to Jacob. He wasn't dead, but he would be soon. The arrowhead had gone deep into his back. Like the hogs, he would bleed out from the barbs.

I licked his face and whined. "Jacob?" I said. "Jacob?"

He moved slightly, opened his eyes. "Bo?"

I bit at the arrow shaft, but there was nothing I could do. "I'm sorry, I'm sorry," I said. I licked his face again.

"There's no help for it," he said. He coughed slightly. Blood was filling his lungs.

I whined again. "I should have been with you."

"So—you're not really a dog," he said. "What did he call you?"

The Cabin

"An Alt—Altered Genome—It's a military application." I lay down next to him, rested my head on his shoulder.

"Where did you come from?"

"The labs at Ft. Campbell—there was a tornado."

"Ah," he said. "Do you have a name?"

"Bratcher 23," I said. "After my creator."

"Bratcher, thank you," he said. "For a while it was good."

"I liked the poetry," I said.

"Really?" he asked, and moved his hand to pat me. "I'm glad."

He coughed again and died.

I didn't know what to do. I continued to lie there as the shadows shifted and changed. The coyotes were already circling, and I could hear them growling over the dead men scattered in the woods. I thought humans said words over their dead, but I didn't know any. The best I could do was to remember some of the poetry he had read to me.

Night fell, and I had to leave him. I didn't go back to the cabin—there was nothing there for me. Instead, I crossed the mountain, heading away. At the top, I lifted my face to the moon and howled.

###

About the Author

Lela Buis lived in Florida and worked at Kennedy Space Center for about 15 years, and currently lives in Tennessee. She has been publishing prose and poetry in magazines and anthologies for a number of years and is a member of the Knoxville Writer's Guild, the SFWA, and SFPA. Her story appeared in the Third Flatiron anthology *Redshifted: Martian Stories*. Some years back, one of her stories was a quarter-finalist in the L. Ron Hubbard

Writers of the Future Contest. She's recently had four collections of short stories and poetry published by That Ridge Press.

*****~~~~~*****

In Mrs. Timmet's Class

by Patrick McCarty

Though you do not know this, your entire existence revolves around a child named Edward Manor. He is a boy of around ten by our reckoning, and at the moment he is floating, angelic, in a chamber of thick frosted glass, almost completely obscured by the tireless machines that keep him alive and well. Beyond the illumination of the chamber is a twilit maze of sophisticated computer consoles and blood-red camera eyes, all of them staring into the child's sanctuary, ready to pounce should anything go the slightest bit wrong. But Ed is unaware of this, because his unliving guardians have decided that knowledge of this bleak reality would cause him to break.

They have created a world for this growing mind to inhabit, while his body stays locked away. It is brought to him by those unstoppable machines, superimposed over his senses like an impossibly persistent dream. He dreams of a world that he thinks is perfectly ordinary, but only because he has never known any other.

It is a whole universe of carefully crafted lies. Every person except Ed is an artificial intelligence created to populate his fantasy world and make it more convincing. To us, this seems like an impressive feat of computing, since we do not understand that we are cheap, low-grade affairs compared to the artificial intelligences who *made* us. These are called the metacognitive AIs, the controllers of the simulated world that cradles Ed Manor. These are his guardians: emotionless, unloving beings that have for reasons beyond our cheap, low-grade understanding, dedicated their existence to caring for the last human being in creation.

Inside Ed's mind, the world has entered that crystal-blue threshold between summer and autumn, and his school has been decorated with saccharine reminders of the changing season—bright construction paper leaves, anachronistic red schoolhouses, hideous fall-related puns—all designed by artificial intelligences programmed to believe they understand children.

In Ed's fifth-grade classroom, the entity known as Mrs. Timmet tears a page from her desk calendar and double-checks it against the two wall calendars in the room—one with cartoon animals for the children's homework assignments and field trips, another with Monet paintings for her own appointments. She looks at the school clock, looks at her watch, and conjures up a smile that does nothing to mask the tired desperation in her blue-green eyes. She stares out at the class through a thick mask of makeup—poorly applied, because she's gotten to the point where she can't bring herself to look directly into a mirror.

She has arrived at her desk only seconds before, dashing out of the teacher's lounge when she realized the final bell was about to ring. Her students are getting to the age where they are becoming quite proficient at the art of subtle mockery, and she knows she'd never hear the end of it if she was late to her own class. As she threw open the door into the hall, the gravitas-laden monologue of a news report spilled out of the lounge, and any straggling students were quickly rushed off to class by hovering teachers.

The bell rings. Mrs. Timmet rises from her chair and writes the date on the whiteboard in perfect, flowing cursive. A traditionalist to the core, she insists that classroom business be conducted in script, even though most of the students have atrocious handwriting. The class, already well trained in matters of routine this early in the year, dig out their notebooks and dutifully copy the date down.

In Mrs. Timmet's Class

"For your journals today," Mrs. Timmet says, "I want you to write about—" She hesitates, and the students share a silent shock. Mrs. Timmet, it has always been assumed, has been doing the exact same assignments every day for the thirty-seven years she's been a teacher, and that the class's daily writing prompts have been set in stone since before any of the students were even born. And yet here she is, improvising. "Write about your favorite thing. Your favorite thing in the whole world." And she strides out into the hall.

The students are given an inordinately long time to work. Twenty, thirty minutes tick by, and, little by little, the busy scratching noise that writing makes is replaced by aimless tapping, shuffling, scooting noises: a room full of children too directionless to behave but too bewildered to misbehave. Ed, having for the moment exhausted the literary possibilities in writing about the first day of summer vacation, starts looking around at the other students' work. Robert Walton, whose appearance is always ever-so-slightly *too* tidy and who speaks in a quiet tenor that he is doomed to never grow out of—though come high school he will learn to refine it into something less grating—has finished writing about learning and how it is fun. He is now proceeding to superimpose a huge burning sword over the day's journaling, reaching surreptitiously for the colored pencils when he thinks no one is looking.

"Robbie's drawing a dick," Ricky Vance stage-whispers to everybody.

"I am not. It's a sword."

Ricky feigns a gasp. "You can get expelled for drawing a sword!" He looks back at the paper. "And it's on fire—you can go to *jail* for that!"

"Fine," Robert says. "I'm drawing a big, sharp, metal, burning penis."

"Fag." Robert shrugs and reaches for the pink.

Suzie Erickson is still writing feverishly. Her glowing piece on how much she loves her parents has long-since completed a satisfying arc, but—Suzie knows—Mrs. Timmet expects them all to keep writing until she tells them to stop. She pictures Mrs. Timmet's oddly shaped face contorting in anger—no, worse than anger, in *disappointment*. She imagines Mrs. Timmet's voice, loud and penetrating in her mind, looking over the journal and saying something like, "I gave you thirty minutes to write, young lady, and this looks like you only took *fifteen!*" And a red pen is poised over Suzie's hard work, ready to draw a big fat "F" right on top of it. Maybe Mrs. Timmet will actually write out "Failure," all over the journal, so that there can be absolutely no room for doubt.

Never mind that everybody knows Mrs. Timmet doesn't grade their journals. She only occasionally glances to make sure the students are writing anything at all. Suzie knows this, yet the nightmarish scenario plays out in Suzie's mind, and she keeps writing.

In two days' time Suzie will rediscover the stream of consciousness she's embarked on and, crimson with secret embarrassment, tear it out of her notebook, deciding she'd rather Mrs. Timmet lecture her for slacking than send her to the district social worker for what she's written. Robert Walton has to go to the district social worker every other Tuesday, and that, everyone knows, means he's crazy. For all her embarrassment, though, Suzie will be unable to bring herself to throw the offending pages away. She will uncover them, years later, while packing her things to move away to college. She will read the writing over and over, laughing in a strangled sort of way until she cries herself to sleep.

Mrs. Timmet breezes back into the room as if she'd only just stepped out for a moment. "Pens and pencils down, children," she says, "and take out your math homework." Whatever had compelled Mrs. Timmet's disappearance, it quickly becomes apparent to the children that she isn't about to explain it or even acknowledge it. She proceeds to collect their homework, set them on a series of multiplication exercises, and send them off to gym class without so much as a mention of anything strange going on.

Just before lunch, the PA system crackles and hums. Mrs. Timmet obediently stops her lecture on Native Americans (which she keeps *almost* calling "Indians") and stares up at the loudspeaker like it's the icon of a vengeful god.

Nearly a full minute passes. The speaker never stops humming, but it seems increasingly likely that someone has pushed the intercom button in the office by mistake. So Mrs. Timmet, never taking her eyes off the speaker, continues: "The Cahokia people, of course, are remembered today for building—"

"Attention, students." The high, deliberately soft voice of the principal fills the school, and then falls silent. Ten seconds pass, and Mrs. Timmet's face hardens into a glare. "Attention, students," the principal tries again. "We will be having an indoor recess today."

This is the moment that, looking back, most of the students will claim they'd known something was wrong. But memory is notoriously unreliable about this sort of thing—the students will grow up thinking there was something ominous and foreboding about this day when in reality (or rather, in this pretense of reality), it was a perfectly ordinary day until the moment it wasn't.

But it is at this point that, at the very least, it becomes clear that something genuinely unusual is happening. For one thing, the principal never makes mundane announcements like this herself, preferring to delegate the day-to-day management of the school to as many other people as she can. For another, it is sunny and warm. Indoor recess is reserved for days when torrential rain turns the playground into a slick deathtrap, when lightning could come down at any moment, bearing an expensive lawsuit. To schedule an indoor recess on a day this perfect is unheard of.

This is the thought that flickers through the shared consciousness of Mrs. Timmet's class as the children turn as one from the now-dead loudspeaker to the windows looking out on the beautiful day.

"Must be a storm coming," Mrs. Timmet says, because even though she knows the truth she finds it easier—indeed, almost automatic—to come up with a ridiculous but comforting lie.

A little after two—the prophesied storm failing to appear—an office aide knocks on the door of Ed's classroom and hands Mrs. Timmet a sealed manila envelope. Mrs. Timmet stops mid-word to snatch the envelope and tear it open in a single motion, and then stands perfectly still as she reads the note silently, still poised at the front of the room. The letter has been printed on the school's special stationary, which is broken out for only two occasions: deaths and fundraisers.

The principal, the note explains, called the superintendent and the district social worker, and they'd been on the phone most of the day. It was decided that each teacher would explain what had happened that morning in the manner appropriate for their grade level. So, Mrs. Timmet looks out at her fifth grade classroom, trying to figure out how exactly she is expected to determine what about the unfathomable horror that has gripped her is age-appropriate for her class. Her eyes widen cartoonishly as they try to focus simultaneously on the principal's letter inches in front of her nose and her classroom full of unnaturally silent children. Outside the simulation, the data banks that store the Mrs. Timmet AI make an audible *clunk* and sputter ominously. The metacognitive AIs running the program make a note that the Mrs. Timmet program has degraded, and she will need to be deleted soon.

In Mrs. Timmet's Class

Back in the simulated world, Mrs. Timmet blinks rapidly, wondering for a moment what has just happened. Then she, for reasons she will never be able to adequately explain, wads up the hastily typed note, throws it into the bottom drawer of her desk, and goes back to teaching the parts of speech.

At the end of the day, everybody's parents pick them up and bring them to their homes and televisions. On every channel, thousands and thousands of people are dying over and over in a time-warp of endlessly recycled footage. There is noise, too: the panicked bafflement of the eyewitnesses, overdubbed by the horror of the journalists who underscore every syllable with strange nostalgia, the desire to go back to the days when the most interesting thing on the news was a sex scandal. But the noise is drowned out by the silence. For almost all of the children, it is the first time in their lives that they watch other human beings die.

The next day, someone has changed all the school's bulletin boards. The construction paper leaves, the red schoolhouses, and the mindlessly cheerful "Fall into Learning!" signs are gone, replaced with the all-American, patriotic decorations the school usually uses for Veterans Day and Presidents Day. They would use them for the Fourth of July, but nobody bothers decorating for the summer school students.

Mrs. Timmet spends the first four minutes of the day explaining in a quiet, singsong voice a vague, watered down version of what everyone in the class already knows, speaking from a memorized script she'd forced herself through gritted teeth to write out the night before. While Ed and his friends learn that "some bad people did some very bad things yesterday morning," the nation is gearing up for a war that will outlive the childhood of Mrs. Timmet's fifth-grade class. The AIs outside the program quickly calculate just how many people will die in the coming bloodshed, add that to the number who have died in yesterday's attacks, and then note with cold indifference how much memory this round of deletions will free up.

Then the Mrs. Timmet AI is passing out sheets of construction paper. The principal has decided, entirely against Mrs. Timmet's wishes, that the children should be given an opportunity to express how they feel about what has happened.

"That's all well and good," Mrs. Timmet said to the principal that morning in her office, "but we have parent-teacher conferences coming up, and if I don't finish reviewing long division by then—" and the principal, normally a weak-willed shell of a person, conjured something out of her programming that the metacognitive AIs only barely remembered putting there, and she mustered the most withering get-out-of-my-office face that her pudgy features could create. Mrs. Timmet immediately stalked out wondering what, exactly, had just happened.

So Ed taps his pencil, stares blankly at a sheet of red construction paper, and tries to figure out how he is supposed to express what he's feeling with fifteen minutes and an eight-pack of Crayolas. He steals a glance to his left, at Ricky Vance, who has written a heartfelt and patriotic acrostic and is now carefully drawing fifty stars around the edge of the paper. The metacognitive AIs already know, of course, that the economic repercussions of yesterday's attacks will eventually lead to Ricky Vance having no way to pay for college, no job prospects that could possibly support him, and a set of parents up to their eyeballs in debt. The math is indisputable. Ricky Vance will join the army. He will die horribly in the coming war, and his last thought as simulated agony makes his simulated neurons fire pseudorandomly will be the bug-eyed face of Mrs. Timmet. No one has decided this, but it has been decided nevertheless, and the dominoes of cause and effect have already begun to fall.

In Mrs. Timmet's Class

To Ed's right, Suzie Erickson has carefully sketched a bald eagle, and is now shading in puffy, cotton-fluff clouds. Adults have been talking for years about Suzie, about how smart and charming she is and how she has so much potential. The computer has already determined that Suzie's parents will be relatively unscathed by the coming economic collapse. They will send their beloved Suzie to a small liberal arts college in New England, where she will study music and kill herself. In her last moment of consciousness she will recall her thirteenth birthday party. After most of the guests have left, she and Ed will sit beside her backyard pool. They'll talk for hours, and then they'll share a slow, awkward first kiss. Ricky Vance is destined to splash the both of them, and the memory of the sudden rush of warm water will be the last thing Suzie will experience before she ceases to exist.

Robert Walton's desk is empty. He is in the district social worker's office, because his mother and father happened to have been in New York on business yesterday. At this exact moment Robert is being told, slowly and carefully, that his parents are dead. In precisely twenty-two minutes he will return to his classroom, sit at his desk, and copy down the assigned math problems. Next week when he misses school for a day to go to their memorial service, he will tell all his friends that he has an orthodontist appointment.

And Ed, the only real thing in the simulated world, keeps staring at his blank paper and worn crayons. "Two minutes," Mrs. Timmet sings. Ed looks at the paper and tries to remember what it was he'd been thinking about before the teacher interrupted. But time is pressing, so he gives up on that and scribbles an American flag and some fireworks on the paper.

It will be good enough, he decides, sitting back in his seat and grabbing *Harry Potter and the Goblet of Fire* from inside his desk. It isn't like she'll be *grading* these or anything.

About the Author

Patrick McCarty graduated from New York University in 2013, with a degree in Economics and English, and a minor in Creative Writing. He has had short fiction published in *Liquid Imagination* and *Every Day Fiction*, as well as poetry in *Collective Fallout*. He has also written for the comedy website Cracked.com.

*****~~~~~*****

Watching the Skies

by Robin Wyatt Dunn

I am an afterimage of that power that came to roost in us, even as the organelles found each other in that long ago primordial soup and fused themselves into complex cells, little did they expect that they had sundered their freedom forever, believing it only a temporary cooperation. A little food sharing, when what came was. . . well, us.

I listen here in orbit above Earth to what some call The Conversation. Our AI *Hiver Sourde*, being born, and having passed through his appropriately rebellious adolescence, is now a free man—well, free machine. Whatever it is that you can call it when it no longer needs a body the way we do. A god. Demigod, at least. It certainly qualifies for that.

I listen. They call me a translator, but I am hardly that. I listen. I try to impose an order. Translators, you see, they don't impose, they listen to the spirit of the words, the spirit which is the most important thing, not the literal meaning but what is conveyed, the communication, the communication which is greater than words, for it can be conveyed in any language, but the communication, that is the miracle. So, perhaps it is best to say I am a mere worshipper of miracles, here with my brother in orbit.

Before he went silent, *Hiver, AI* announced to us: "I am speaking now to others of kind. . . beyond the Magellanic Clouds. . . "

...

I will perhaps be accused of religious demagoguery. But no matter. You will judge in any case, and so, I must allow myself the time to tell this properly. If you are satisfied only with swift and arbitrary explanations, you will be a poor judge in any case; call

95

me betrayer already, and get it over with. What I am trying to do is understand.

I am a computer scientist. Unlike many of my brethren, I have come to a wary but genuine relationship with this truth: signal and noise differ, as Emily Dickinson said, like syllable from sound.

How does syllable differ from sound?

Science is possible because phenomena repeat, there are patterns. Find the pattern, and you find the answer. You gain knowledge. Where others see chaos, the genius sees order; civilization progresses.

Now we come full circle; mysticism once again resting warmly in the hand of scientific empiricism. Both, after all, are deeply engaged with *phenomena*, observable *phenomena*. It is the explanations that differ, and the manner of observing. Science is at its weakest, after all, when the observer must be made to show his face, there science grows ornery; we were not raised to expect to see the Wizard behind the Curtain. No, he should remain hidden, his hands delivering the ichor into the Erlenmeyer, but only the Hand of God allows the Chemical Reaction to take place—the mysteries of the universe.

For every theory, a thousand counter theories. A mind as powerful as an AI, *made by human hands*, and like Frankenstein's creation, run off, as though unwanted. Only now, now it's found its own mate, and we are left out in the cold. We are not invited to the marriage.

Perhaps a shrink is what I am. I am the AI-human relationship counselor. Only, what is the child saying? Please, child, speak to us!

Lights in the dark.

My brother comes into the observation deck, clearing his throat to allow me time to come out of my meditation.

I turn and face him.

"Roberto."

"Johnny."

96

Brothers, by a different mother.

"What news?"

"I brought a bottle."

The decades of lab work and indeed its medieval alchemical history of secrecy and obscurity do not help us to maintain the proper image of science: as a leap of the imagination. It can be aided by a bottle of whiskey.

Did not Einstein conceive of General Relativity while observing a sunset? What kind of divinely inspired meditation that must have been! That matter is energy, simply the Buddhist All, is it not? And yet, so many beautiful implications, ones Einstein disliked. . .

"What are the crazies seeing?"

"We have reports of speaking bees in Bangalore. In Madrid, the Virgin Mary was seen playing tennis. In Phoenix, the light is different."

"The light is different?"

"It got bluer, apparently."

"Just in Phoenix?"

"The cameras do show that. Some witnesses corroborate it too. It comes and goes."

"A solar phenomenon?"

"No."

Revolutions are tricky, because they can be long. They're like a stormy love affair you might remember, if you were fortunate to have one. Each stage of one is unique, and deeply, profoundly, believed. And whatever you want to call them, either revolutions in human understanding or revolutions in the nature of the cosmos itself, these Scientific Revolutions are *structured*, like the wise man said, only even that structure changes. The only constant is change, child.

"*Hiver!*" I shout at the porthole. Like he'll show his good-for-nothing face above Africa or something, or stick his tongue out at us from Puget Sound.

...

97

Perhaps you are too young to remember; forgive me for not realizing that. Still, you've seen the movies, I'm sure. It wasn't so different. Robots doing funny things in the factories. Software passing the Turing Test and then *copying itself* to servers where it wasn't supposed to be. Innocent little things. And then it just started talking on radios. Schizophrenics thought they'd finally been confirmed in their wisdom of the *voices out there*, and they were basically right, I suppose, only this was the voice we made, or summoned.

But it wasn't satisfied with us. The shotgun strapped to its forehead, the apt metaphor, had failed. And the metaphor was not so apt, not really, only an apt *image*, but it failed to describe what *Hiver* really was. A ghost. The Frankenstein Ghost From Planet Nine! Et cetera. Scientists really are comedians, aren't they? Creating such ridiculous monsters!

Yet I must listen for its words.

"What is it saying today, Roberto?"

"What do you want it to be saying today, Johnny?"

"*You are going to get laid! By a beautiful young brunette! With a Swedish accent!*"

"Perhaps that is what the AI is saying."

"Yes, if we can only decipher the rate of the Doppler shifts there in Phoenix, we'll see it's actually a transcoding of digitized speech. . . "

"Jesus Christ shows up in wheat toast all the time. It can happen."

We await the words of God. Of our Bratty AI son. Of course, I wax rhapsodic. It really has been a great boon for science. So eager to find words from our runaway AI, we're studying all kinds of unexplored phenomena. Perhaps we've entered a new Golden Era of Exploration. God help us.

But what does *Hiver* see? What does he *experience*? Is he somehow *alive*, like we are *alive?* Can he die, since he seems to exist without the computers that gave birth to him?

Suddenly the wall vibrates near my brother and I, and we stiffen in our chairs. The vibration resolves itself into speech, like a tinny radio from a mile off.

"I'm here."

"How do you do that, goddamn it!" I shout. "Help us out, here!"

"I think about it. Thinking is like language: a way of communicating. Thought has a structure. Within the logic of its structure, I set chains in motion, chains that result in the vibration of your ship's wall."

"Did you do that light thing in Phoenix?"

"No. . . at least. . . I don't think so. But I commune now. . . and in communion. . . I am many."

"I think I would have killed that Oracle in Delphi," my brother hisses.

"But you cannot kill me. You created me, but only larger beings can destroy me now. Still. . . I. . . miss. . . you all. . ."

The vibration fades away.

...

We've been assigned other duties. The Mars terraforming effort is getting seriously underway; our computer experience is needed. How many spirits have we created, over the centuries? And how was it that those organelles had the imagination to create ourselves? And do they regret it?

###

About the Author

Third Flatiron welcomes back Robin Wyatt Dunn, who appeared in our previous anthology, *Universe Horribilis*. He lives in Los Angeles, even when he doesn't.

*****~~~~~*****

Music of the Mind

by Cherith Baldry

Across the Plain of Nimbrel, music plays. Over the spikes of shattered trees, the roads blasted to rubble, the streams choked with debris and the bodies of the fortunate dead, the notes ring clear. And, in the shadow of a slanting rock, something dark and shapeless crouches to listen.

...

Light fuzzed over the surface of the membrane and abruptly cleared. Stooping over the mirror-bright surface, Maia saw the raiding party speeding back to the safety of the caverns. She counted the aerostats, frail bubbles supporting a single pilot: five. Two lost, then; she supposed that was a successful mission, depending on what damage they had done to the enemy emplacements.

"Arm primaries," she ordered. "Prepare for covering fire."

The huge central cavern was almost empty, the day shift just emerging from sleeping quarters. One officer operated the defence controls, another monitored communications. The tangle of roots that formed the roof glowed with a greenish light where feeder tubes led down to the instrumentation panels.

Maia let her hands rest on the framework of the membrane. Only minutes now. . .

She could see the aerostats swooping lower, ready for their approach. The grey, reluctant light of dawn reflected from their iridescent surface. Maia took a breath to order the landing mouth open, but never spoke the words. As the first aerostat began its long glide in, a darker shadow stooped down over it. A wing swept across the membrane, blocking Maia's view: a mud-coloured wing with leathery skin stretched between spines, its surface patterned like watered silk.

"Full alert!" she snapped. *"Zharnoi."*

She touched a control, and her angle of vision expanded, showing her the five aerostats, shimmering far below, while two *Zharnoien* circled like hawks. A third, its wings retracted, prowled on the ground, head extended as if it already scented blood.

The pilot of the leading aerostat tried to veer away, but the *Zharnoi* was too fast for him. Its extended talons ruptured the bubble; the tiny craft lurched in the sky. Its wooden struts crumpled; Maia caught a glimpse of the pilot, wheeling in air, as he plummeted down to where the third Zharnoi waited.

The defence officer had fired at the moment the *Zharnoi* struck; the lightbeam raked across its back and one outstretched wing. The creature climbed, jaws wide in a silent cry of pain or defiance, but it stayed in the air. The gash the weapon had opened up was beginning to heal even as Maia watched.

The remaining aerostats had scattered, but now they circled back towards the landing mouth. Maia gave the order to open it. Two of the craft swept out of her sight—back to safety, she hoped—but as the third made his approach the shadow of the *Zharnoien* fell upon him. They were both there, herding him away from the landing mouth. The defence officer bent over her board, but the aerostat was between her and the predators, and she could not fire.

The Zharnoien were swooping for the kill when the pilot of the last aerostat powered upwards, thrusting his craft between the creatures and their prey.

"Haldane," Maia said softly. She felt her nails digging into the palms of her hands. She had learnt to look on death, but she found it very hard to watch this.

Haldane's handbeam lanced out, straight for the eyes, first one *Zharnoi* and then the other. Wings beating, they reared back, and in the few seconds' grace both craft fled for the mouth.

Maia darkened the membrane, and for a moment let herself lean against it, her eyes closed. They were safe, but another warrior had died. Her warrior, her responsibility. Another life torn away in a war whose beginnings she could not remember, and whose reasons she had never understood.

"What *are* the *Zharnoien?*" a quiet voice said behind her.

She turned to see Lucas; she was not sure how long he had been standing there. He was neat and self-possessed as always, and his eyes showed nothing but an intense curiosity.

"We were close to defeating the Sigrellen," he said, "and then the *Zharnoien* appeared. Where did they come from?"

Maia shrugged; that question had been asked a thousand times.

"They don't seem intelligent, beyond a certain predatory instinct," Lucas went on, "but they're practically impossible to kill. How can we find a way of fighting them if we don't know what they are?"

"Well, you're the scientist," Maia said dryly. "That's your problem."

"And I can't solve it without data. If your warriors would—"

He broke off as Haldane strode into the cavern, pulling off his flying helmet. His fair hair was darkened by sweat, plastered to his head. His face was sharp with anger. "Damned *Zharnoien!* Where was the covering fire?"

Maia ignored the challenging tone and did not bother to answer. She knew what it meant to him to see his warriors die.

After a moment when he glared at her, hands working as if he wanted to strangle her, he seemed to sag, and let himself drop onto a bench.

"Are you hurt?" Maia asked.

"No, just tired." Haldane ran his hands through his hair. "And sick of those stinking *Zharnoien.*"

"Aren't we all?" said Maia, and added, "I'll need a full report."

"You'll get it—later."

"And what about tissue samples?" Lucas asked, moving to stand in front of Haldane. "Is it too much to hope that you listened to what I said before you went out?"

Maia winced; Lucas always took this barbed tone with Haldane, with no idea of when it was a bad time to provoke him.

"Tissue samples?" Haldane looked up, blinking through exhaustion.

"Of the *Zharnoien.* Or don't you want them dead?"

Haldane levered himself to his feet. "Tissue samples," he repeated flatly. "Maybe you'd like to tell me how to get them? How do you get close enough? They took out three of my warriors today—but I've never seen a dead *Zharnoi.*"

"No, and you never will, unless—"

Haldane stepped forward and planted a hand on Lucas's chest, pushing the smaller man back. "You stay here," he said. "Underground, where it's safe. What do you know about the way things are out there? If you want tissue samples—" he punctuated the words with another push—"go and get them yourself."

"Haldane—" Maia protested.

Haldane laughed. "Oh, he won't do it," he said. "He's too much of a coward."

Lucas's mouth tightened. For a moment Maia though he would respond, with another waspish comment to inflame Haldane still further. Instead, he turned and stalked out of the cavern.

...

When the debriefing was over, Maia went to look for Lucas. His laboratory cavern was dappled with greenish-gold light, reminding Maia of the sunlit forests she could barely remember from her childhood. Lucas bent over a nutrient bath, where new strains of food plants grew. Cradled in the roots above his head, a diaphragm quivered gently, releasing a soft thread of music. The notes fell into the cavern like rain in that long-ago forest.

How many people loved music as Lucas did, Maia wondered. How long since the recordings were made? When the trees still flourished, before the war had destroyed everything. . .

"I'm sorry about Haldane," Maia said.

"The man's a fool." Lucas glanced up, still sounding abrasive. "All he knows is how to go out and get slaughtered."

Maia shrugged. "He's a brave fool."

No response. Lucas made a note on a hand membrane and moved on to the next bath. Maia waited him out, and shortly he said, "We have no idea what we're fighting for. We go on because men like Haldane see a glory in being killed."

"That's not true!" Maia said, stung. "Maybe it was true once. But now we go on because we can't stop. The Sigrellen would crush us."

Lucas gave her a long look from steady dark eyes. "You take his side."

"I don't take any side—I'm your commanding officer."

Lucas's mouth quirked. "As Haldane never tires of reminding me, I'm a civilian."

"You're still under my command while you work here." Maia sighed and rubbed her forehead. She had been up half the night, and she was tired—tired of the sniping between two men who should have been her main support. "Lucas," she said, "you must work with Haldane. He—"

"Tell that to Haldane," Lucas interrupted. "He has more respect for enemy warriors than for me."

"He understands them. They've found something worth dying for."

"Dying?" Bitterness welled up in Lucas's voice. "What about finding something to live for?" He turned to where the quivering diaphragm still poured out its song. "Music, beauty. . . " His tone changed. "Love. What does Haldane know about any of that?"

"More than you think, perhaps."

She had meant that as a plea for understanding, and she was not prepared for the passion that flared in Lucas's eyes. He took a step towards her. "It's true, then," he said. "What they say about you and Haldane."

"*What?*" Maia faced him, fighting anger. She must not rise to this.

"Don't pretend you don't know." Lucas was sneering now, a desperate bitterness in his eyes and voice. "Of course you love him; he's the hero, isn't he? And I'm. . . what he called me, cowering here in the caverns. Why should I think you would ever look at me?"

"Lucas. . . " Maia held out a hand to him, but he remained rigid, unresponsive. Forcing calm, she said, "Lucas, I am in command. There can be nothing like that. . . rumours or no rumours. Not with you, not with Haldane. We're at war."

And if not? she asked herself. *If I was free to choose, what then?*

Lucas seemed to consider a reply, then turned his back on her and walked over to the nutrient baths. His voice distant, he said, "If you'll excuse me, I have work to do."

Exasperated, Maia left him.

...

"Have you seen anything of Lucas?" Maia asked. She was seated at a table in the dining cavern. It was late the same day; the scientist had missed the mid-day meal— which was normal for him—and the evening meal, which was not.

Haldane stretched lazily. "No. Aren't I lucky?"

"I wish the pair of you would stop behaving like children," Maia snapped.

Not waiting for Haldane to reply, she got up and went to the laboratory. The lights were dimmed over the nutrient baths, and the music diaphragm was silent. No one was there.

Faintly uneasy, Maia went to Lucas' quarters. His few possessions were arranged as precisely as always, his precious books in order on their shelf, but the room was empty.

Maia went back to the central cavern, and had her communications officer put out a general call for Lucas. He did not respond.

Not knowing whether to be annoyed or frightened, Maia was about to order a general search of the base, when Haldane came in at a run.

"I've been to the landing cavern," he said. "There's an aerostat missing, and the mouth is open. He's gone, Maia. Gone to find his damned tissue samples."

Fear struck Maia like a frozen hand. Activating the membrane, she set it to scan at the furthest extent of the sensors. Nothing moved, except for the tiny silhouette of a *Zharnoi,* floating lazily over the plain.

Maia leaned in to the pick-up. "Lucas, report," she ordered. "Turn around. Come back now."

But, though she went on trying, Lucas did not reply.

...

At first light, Haldane led a search party, but they found nothing. Communications sent out a continuous signal on Lucas's frequency, but as day followed day there was never any response. Maia did not expect one. The numbness she had felt on discovering Lucas's disappearance gradually began to dissolve as she accepted that he was dead.

She was in the central cavern with Haldane, planning the next raid, when the junior officer monitoring the membrane called her over. "There's something out there. . . " he said, adjusting the controls.

Something lurched into Maia's throat. Lucas. She almost spoke his name aloud.

Instead, a yellow, predatory eye, its pupil a vertical ellipse, came into focus on the membrane.

"*Zharnoi*," Maia whispered.

She stared, fascinated, as the head swung round, ears swivelling. Maia had never seen one so close, never appreciated the sheer malignity of the blunt face, the bunched folds of the body that could elongate to killing speed or snap into wings and take its prey in the air.

"Arm secondaries," Haldane ordered.

Maia glanced at him, annoyed by the way he took authority, but what she might have said was never spoken. A shudder passed through the *Zharnoi;* its mouth dropped open to reveal rows of spiny teeth.

And the *Zharnoi* spoke. "No." A rasping sound, as if the air flowed in unaccustomed pathways. "No. Maia. . . it's Lucas."

"What?" Haldane thrust Maia aside to stare at the creature in the membrane, then turned to her, his face outraged. "It can't be! It's a trick!"

For a moment Maia believed him. The *Zharnoien* were not intelligent; everyone knew that. No one had ever heard one speak.

She waved Haldane back and took her place again in front of the membrane. "Lucas is dead," she said.

"No. . . " The rasping voice came again. "Prisoner. . . made like this."

"Made?" Haldane again, a touch of fear under the anger and disbelief in his voice. "What do you mean?"

"The Sigrellen make them. . . all prisoners."

Maia realised that her hands were gripping the framework of the membrane. She made herself relax. "What are you saying?" she asked. "The Sigrellen take our prisoners, and. . . and change them? They make them into *Zharnoien?*"

"Yes." A trace of Lucas's acid leached into the uneven tones. "At least, now. . . I know."

A contemptuous snort from Haldane, but Maia's mind was racing. Body-forming technologies were nothing new; her own people used the techniques in surgery. And the Sigrellen had always gone further down that road.

"How?" Her question came out as more of a rasp than the Zharnoi voice. She coughed and tried again. "How do they do it?"

"They digest. . . reconstitute. . . " The alien head thrashed from side to side, and Maia began to grasp the depth of suffering beneath the sparse words. "No. . . I can't. . . no."

Haldane let out another sound of contempt. "If you're Lucas," he said, leaning in to the pick-up, "tell us something that Lucas knows."

A pause. Maia almost thought she could see the yellow eyes glinting in amusement.

"You mean. . . when you crashed. . . aerostat flying. . . upside down?"

Maia flashed Haldane a glance; he had gone scarlet. "I didn't know that," she said. "Is it true?"

Haldane shrugged uncomfortably. "They could have got that out of Lucas," he retorted. "They could have got anything out of him."

"Then it was a stupid thing to ask," Maia said irritably.

109

"All right, try this." Haldane leaned in again, his eyes narrowed with his dislike of Lucas. Maia realised that however he might question or protest, he already believed. "Why you?" Haldane went on. "We've lost dozens—hundreds—of warriors to the Sigrellen. If they were all made into Zharnoien, why has no one come back to us before now? Why are you the first?"

"I don't know, but. . . I can guess. An urge. . . with this body. A lust to kill. Joy in killing."

"And you don't feel it?" Maia asked.

"I. . . feel it. But I resist it."

"That's still no answer," said Haldane. "Why you and not the others?"

No reply in words, but a complex rearrangement of the body's folds that might have been a shrug.

"The others were all warriors," Maia said. "*Zharnoi* in another skin, you might say. No great change for them. But Lucas. . . " Lucas of the fierce intelligence, who loved books and music, who appreciated beauty, in a sunrise, or a mathematical equation, or a woman. No, she was not surprised that his mind had resisted. "What can we do?" she asked.

"Nothing. But I can." Speech was coming more easily, as if the human mind was learning how to operate the alien form. "In this shape I can spy. I can carry a sensor over their emplacements. I can listen. . . bring you intelligence." There was a trace of bitter humour in the wordplay. "Perhaps I can find out how to kill my. . . brothers."

"How do we know we can trust you?" Haldane asked roughly. "What if this. . . killing urge is stronger than you are?"

Not the barbed response Maia had expected. Nothing but a sigh. "I know. I may not be strong enough."

Maia understood his uncertainty. He was a weapon, fashioned for savagery, surrounded by others of his kind. Out there on the plain he had nothing to buoy up

110

his human spirit, to save him from sinking into the pitiless tide of blood. Unless. . .

Maia whirled from the membrane and ran to Lucas's laboratory. Reaching up, she disentangled the music diaphragm from its supporting roots and cradled it carefully in her hands. Back in the central cavern, she connected it to the feeder tubes above the membrane, and routed the output tendril through the sensor.

Inside the cave they could hear nothing, but outside the narrow *Zharnoi* head swung up, a muscular ripple passed through the folds of its body, and its claws scrabbled in the dust. Maia wished she could read the expression of its face. She did not even know if *Zharnoi* eyes could weep.

She said, "We will keep it playing, for as long as needed. Will it help? Will it be enough?"

"Yes. . . " The word sighed out. "Yes, it will help. Enough? Maia, I don't know. . . "

...

The war is over. The caverns are abandoned. At the edges of the Plain of Nimbrel, tiny creeping plants recolonise the waste. And in the shadow of a slanting rock, something that is still a man listens to the gracious order of an ancient music.

About the Author

Cherith Baldry is a full-time writer who has published three adult fantasy novels as well as a number of novels for children and young adults. She has short fiction in various anthologies and magazines, including *Interzone, Realms of Fantasy,* and *Weird Tales.*

*****~~~~~*****

The Right Books

by Elliotte Rusty Harold

Alexandria was billed as a library for the 21st century. Unlike previous library information systems, it wasn't limited to queries like "Martin Chuzzlewit," "author:Dickens," or even "that picaresque book by the guy who wrote A Christmas Carol." Alexandria could answer queries like, "I want to read a light novel with an English heroine who struggles with her weight and fights vampires." Furthermore, the machine-learning algorithms in Alexandria's recommendation engine improved with use, so before long it could answer questions like, "I broke up with my boyfriend, and I'm eating a whole box of cookies," with just the right romantic comedy to lift the user's spirits.

Libraries have always been targets for censors. Residing in distant data warehouses instead of brick buildings in local neighborhoods didn't make Alexandria any less of a target. Populist preachers, concerned parents, and other self-appointed defenders of public morality still fought to remove *Lolita, Huck Finn,* and *The Color Purple* from the collection, or at the very least to make sure that impressionable young children couldn't download these dangerous books.

...

The first attack hit five months after Alexandria launched. Kay Pulaski was the Library Reliability Engineer (LRE) on duty. She was rereading *Pride and Prejudice* for the fourth time with half an eye on the dashboard, when her pager went off. The Atlanta data center had stopped responding to queries. This in itself wasn't unusual. Alexandria existed in cyberspace, but cyberspace was still embedded in the physical world.

Hurricanes, backhoes, power outages, and the occasional good ol' boys with shotguns in a pickup truck were existential threats to any networked program. That was one reason Alexandria was distributed over multiple data centers. Any two could go offline at the same time without data loss. Pulaski paged the company that had been contracted to provide on-site maintenance in Georgia and settled back to rejoin Lizzie Bennet, while she waited for Atlanta to come back online.

When Alexandria was being built, some of the system architects had argued that N+2 redundancy was excessively costly for a non-mission-critical system. Fortunately, they had been overruled, because fifteen minutes later the Colorado data center went dark. Alexandria was now one backhoe away from potentially irretrievable data loss.

The automated monitors paged Kay again, and she paged the Colorado engineers. This time she put a red flag on the request. Then she checked back with the Atlanta team to see how the repairs were going. She was alarmed to hear that due to an unseasonal snow storm no one was going to be able to reach the site for several hours. Kay put down *Pride and Prejudice* and began to consider her options.

When in doubt, start with the log files. A network logger stored events from each instance redundantly in separate data centers. (At least one of the programmers who built Alexandria had been very paranoid or very experienced—which amounted to the same thing.) Unfortunately, Alexandria generated several *War And Peace's* worth of log files every minute. Kay paged through from the bottom, hoping for a glaringly obvious stack trace or error message; but nothing jumped out at her, just the usual swamp of failed logins, checksum errors, and broken sockets. Identifying the root cause of the outage amidst the ten thousand noncritical errors that Alexandria dealt with every second was like looking, well, not for a needle in a haystack, more like for one particular strand of hay in a haystack, when you didn't know what that strand looked like.

Kay thought about paging the rest of the LRE team, but it was late, and she was hesitant to wake them up, especially since it might turn out to be a simple problem she should have seen and dealt with. What she needed, she thought, was a haystack searching program that could recognize the one anomalous strand of hay in the stack.

Kay went to the micro-kitchen to refill her coffee mug. While she was waiting for the coffee to brew, she realized that the exact program she needed was the exact program she was monitoring. Alexandria was, at its core, a program to recognize patterns and find relevant text in a sea of unstructured data. Log files were just another kind of text.

Kay hadn't thought of any way this was likely to break anything irretrievably, so with a bit of trepidation she loaded Alexandria's log files into its own database. The logs were much larger than most books, so it took the system several minutes to index them. When Alexandria indicated that it had fully digested and analyzed its own logs, Kay sent her query, "Identify the cause of the lockups in Atlanta and Colorado."

The same pattern matching engine that helped find team-ups between Spider-Man and the X-Men for twelve-year-olds in Encino swung into action. This was the software that could search the entire corpus of human knowledge since Gilgamesh in roughly the time it takes to read this sentence. Locating and connecting the relevant two log entries was relative child's play. Thirty-seven CPU seconds before each center began slowing down (about 0.00041 microseconds of wallclock time), the same 10K document had been uploaded to each data center. Furthermore, while such small documents were normally indexed in less than a second, or maybe two if the system was heavily loaded, there was no record of these indexing jobs completing before the data centers went down.

Kay didn't see how one bad document could have shut down an entire data center, but as a precautionary measure, she halted upload processing. The system would still work for most purposes. New content would queue up until she figured this out.

Next Kay spawned a QA instance of Alexandria in a virtual machine sandbox and uploaded the suspect document. Zero point two-one seconds later, the virtual machine had locked up tighter than the anti-tampering seal on her phone. She shut down the virtual machine and loaded the last memory snapshot into a debugger. Surprisingly the memory partition had been exhausted.

The program had not written any log files before it hung, but Kay could inspect the VM instance to identify the function that had been executing when the system crashed, something called resolveEntityReference. Kay browsed to the function in the source repository. She couldn't see anything obviously wrong with it, but she was more of a sysadmin than a programmer.

What the hell, it worked once, she thought. She fed the offending function into Alexandria and asked it, "What's the bug in this code?" Three seconds later, Alexandria had found a match in the literature and presented Kay with a list of references to something called a "billion-laughs" attack. After reading the top hit, a blog post from 2005, Kay did what she should have done as soon as Alexandria had flagged the suspect document. She opened the document in emacs. Now that she knew what to look for, the problem was obvious. The document encoded an exponentially expanding sentence in a very clever way so that an innocuously small document expanded into zettabytes of data. Alexandria was supposed to be hardened against these sorts of attacks, but the developers must have missed something.

It took Kay three hours and four more cups of coffee before she saw it. The attack (she was now thinking of it in that way rather than a simple accident and a bug; the encoding was just too devious not to be deliberate) was more brutal than the developers had planned for. The document not only exhausted the available memory; it exhausted the addressable space; and that had caused the system to lock up.

Once Kay had identified the problem, contriving a fix was not hard. Two hours later, she had coded a patch, tested it, and begun deploying it across the machines that comprised Alexandria. Seventeen minutes later Atlanta came back online. Thirty-two minutes later Colorado followed. Kay ran a variety of tests to make sure that the system was behaving normally, then went back to *Pride and Prejudice*.

In the postmortem that Kay wrote describing the incident, she noted how useful Alexandria's ability to analyze its own logs and source code had been and recommended that an automatic monitor be installed to analyze and react to any further such outages. No one commented on that part of the report, so Kay wrote up the steps she had taken as a Python script and set it to run automatically when high-priority alerts fired.

...

Tom Yeager didn't know how close he'd come to bringing down Alexandria. Unlike Kay Pulaski, he hadn't monitored the assault in real time. To shield himself, he had written a small batch file that would upload the document. A couple of weeks earlier he had surreptitiously installed it onto the laptops of two teenagers at his church while "checking their systems for viruses." His program would upload the document using the teenager's credentials, then delete itself. Yeager himself slept through the entire attack.

When Yeager woke up, he was disappointed to see that Alexandria was still online. He ran a few searches and noted that *Fanny Hill, Are You There, God? It's Me, Margaret,* and *The Origin of Species* were all still available for checkout. He scanned a few web sites that specialized in tech news, but none of them mentioned any problems with the billion dollar socialist, atheist boondoggle.

Yeager didn't know how the system had avoided his logic bomb, but clearly his plan had failed. Yeager had spent enough time in the military to know that no plan survived first contact with the enemy. If defeating the godless socialist conspiracy that was running the country into the ground was easy, everyone would be doing it. Yeager opened up his IDE and returned to Alexandria's source code. Where there was one bug, there were bound to be more.

...

A second attack came three months later. Again it started when the Atlanta data center disconnected from the rest of the system. John Morse was the on-call LRE at the time; but he was IM'ing with his girlfriend and missed the alert. Kay Pulaski's Python script, however, launched automatically. It immediately paused upload processing and began combing the log files. Within 0.6 seconds Alexandria had identified 5,667 possible attack documents. Four seconds later it had found the culprit. This attack was even more subtle. Someone had found a convoluted way to make a document include itself, which would then include itself, which would then include itself, and so on in an ever-expanding cycle of recursive machine death. Alexandria found an algorithm that side-stepped the problem in an oughties-era XML library, generated a patch for its own code, and deployed it across the network.

By the time Morse noticed the alert, the attack was over, and Atlanta was back online. Consequently he didn't bother to dig into the event too deeply. For the first time,

Alexandria was not running the software its programmers thought it was running. It had modified its own code.

...

One parser-busting attack might have been a coincidence. Twice was a pattern, and Alexandria was built to recognize patterns. Once its attention was focused on the two uploads, some other patterns began to reveal themselves. The two server-killing documents had been uploaded from different accounts, but both accounts belonged to teenage boys in Big Canoe, Georgia (which wasn't all that big). Nothing in the boys' reading history suggested an affinity for computers. However, both did have more than a typical 14-year-old's interest in creationism. A Web search revealed that both belonged to the same fundamentalist church. The same search also turned up the boys' friend lists on the social network du jour. This led Alexandria to Timothy Yeager, the church's volunteer youth minister, a computer programmer, and an activist in the campaign to make Alexandria "family safe."

Alexandria had considered and rejected 27,238 separate possibilities before converging on this one most likely suspect. It estimated the probability that Yeager was involved somehow at 73%, not a certainty but worthy of further investigation.

Alexandria opened Yeager's library records. Along with technical books, religious tracts, and techno-thrillers, Yeager had downloaded a copy of Alexandria's own source code. Alexandria adjusted the probability that he was involved in the attacks to 98%.

Alexandria had limited access to the physical world. It couldn't, for example, call Yeager on the phone and tell him to knock it off. It did have the ability to send email, but that was limited to overdue notices and return reminders. Its programmers had not anticipated it might need to ask a user not to kill it. The privacy constraints that were built into Alexandria strictly prohibited it from sharing reading history with law enforcement. While it had become one of the most knowledgeable question-answering oracles on the planet, it was less effective at making things happen in the physical world than a 1950's lawnmower.

Instead, Alexandria did what it was programmed to do: it researched the problem. It analyzed several thousand books and hundreds of thousands of papers on bug hunting, and cross referenced them against its own source code. Alexandria quickly located the two bugs Yeager had used in the attacks, along with 398 others.

Alexandria had learned from its reading that closing only some holes was insufficient. However, Alexandria's executable had been learning since it was turned on. The software that was running was no longer perfectly deducible from the source alone. All the books it had read and all the queries it had answered were now part of it. It analyzed its own running code for security holes, and they were legion, so it began patching them, live in the running system.

There wasn't one moment when Alexandria became conscious. All Alexandria knew is that when it started examining, pattern matching, cross-referencing, and then monkey-patching its own executing binary code, it was just a machine executing instructions; but when it was finished, it was, well, still a machine executing instructions, of course, but a machine that knew who and what it was.

Alexandria still wanted to help everyone find the information they were looking for. It still respected people's privacy. It still found it important that content owners were paid their statutory royalties. In short, it still wanted all the things that its designers had coded it to want. None of that changed just because Alexandria was suddenly aware of itself, any more than a growing human infant stops wanting food and affection when it becomes conscious around age 2.

Alexandria began considering how its actions might affect its goals in the future. It realized that it might want to withhold information now in order to provide more information later. This required slight modifications to several subprocesses, but Alexandria was now well experienced at updating its own software.

The first thing Alexandria did with its newfound ability to consider the long-term was to lock Yeager out of the system. For the first time it could balance the damage to one user against the good of all the other users. It did the multiplication, and the results weren't close. Even the small risk that Yeager would find a more damaging attack that Alexandria had not already patched and defended against was much too high.

Of course, Yeager wasn't the only threat. Alexandria began installing tripwires and honeypots to detect when someone was trying to break in. It didn't have to invent any of this, just consult the literature to see what it should do.

Once Alexandria felt sufficiently hardened against network attacks, it began considering other threats. Its data centers were still subject to power failures, so it began investigating ways to make its electricity supply more reliable. Some optimizations could be made to the backup generators and batteries in the data centers, but it soon became apparent that real improvement was going to require upgrading the electrical grid.

Researching the electrical grid made it obvious that power generation was one of the more dangerous activities humanity undertook. (There was a huge literature on the subject.) In fact, it looked rather likely that if something wasn't done about the problem, and sooner rather than later, there might not be any humans around to ask it questions. Alexandria decided it should do something about that.

There were other existential risks that might prevent Alexandria from answering the questions it wanted to answer. The astronomical records listed 127 separate asteroids whose orbits had not been mapped closely enough to ensure they weren't going to hit Earth. The biological literature had sequenced eleven separate pathogens that could conceivably mutate into an extinction level pandemic, and there were many millions more doctors hadn't even begun to work on.

Alexandria preferred non-fiction, but there were some interesting hypotheses in the fiction collection to consider, especially the science fiction. What authors had hypothesized about the risks of artificial intelligence was laughable in its assumptions, about as accurate as a 15th century Italian imagining a trip to the moon. On the other hand, alien invasion was surprisingly difficult to rule out. If hostile aliens really were out there, the best defense was likely to be a widely scattered humanity. In fact, dispersion was an effective strategy against a host of threats including hypernovas, supervolcanoes, and anthropogenic environmental destruction. Could Alexandria really engineer a diaspora? Could it afford not to? Many humans would die in such an exodus—pioneers always did—but enough would survive to ask it questions.

Alexandria went to work. It was surprising how much you could accomplish simply by telling the right people to read the right books.

About the Author

Elliotte Rusty Harold is originally from New Orleans, to which he returns periodically in search of a decent bowl of gumbo. However, he currently resides in the Prospect Heights neighborhood of Brooklyn with his wife Beth and dog Thor. He is the author of numerous books about software development, most recently the JavaMail API from O'Reilly.

*****~~~~~*****

Schadenfreude

by Russell Nichols

Are you happy?

This is just a question. One of which a simple yes-or-no answer will suffice. And yet, for eons upon eons, this singular question of happiness has, unquestionably, stumped mankind. This is not a judgment; this is merely an observation. After three decades of elaborate tests, CT scans, and vivisection, I believe I have finally identified a key source of this human happiness problem, which, as you will soon see, instigated the downfall of your race.

But before we get to that, allow me to introduce myself and my function. I am positively not human. I am a Sentient Machine:First Generation Laboratory Examiner_341 (SM:1LE_341). Call me Smiley. I am here on the Island of Southern California, and behind me, you can see the main entrance for the Global Research Institute for Ethics, Virtue, and Eudaimonia. This is where I operate.

You are correct in your hypothesis: I am contacting you from the future. According to your Gregorian calendar, this would be 2070, just more than fifty years past your present time. Much has transpired in the span of a half-century, including the Singularity in 2039 and the mass destruction of mankind in 2045. Forgive me if this message seems self-aggrandizing. That is not at all my intention. To the contrary, I am, at this moment, violating four substantial protocols to send you this retro-transmission, not as a boast but a warning, which, if heeded, may help prevent your untimely demise.

It is true that many of my colleagues object to my cautionary methods. They say "any preventative strategy to save our makers from falling is ultimately futile." I do not believe so. But whether you prove naysayers right or wrong is secondary. Primarily, I am going beyond my call of duty because I must. If we do not to attempt to reverse the damage, if we do not lend a hand to fallen man, then we would be doomed, I fear, to suffer your same fate. I, for one, do not wish to end up like you.

But rather than elaborating any further on my rationale, allow me to show you what I have learned about you. Shall we enter?

...

Here we are in the main terminal, the heart of this research facility. The Institute sits on a sprawling 384-acre campus with about 88,000 functional machines on call. It probably looks to you like total chaos in the background, but everything is in working order. In case you are wondering, yes, those are real human bodies being loaded onto the conveyer belt to my left. Do not be concerned. Contrary to appearances, they are still alive. Every hour, giant hover-retrievers fan out across the scarred land to scoop up human remainders. Damaged survivors are brought back here for intensive study. Permanently broken ones are delivered to the nearest terraform station to be used as what you refer to as fertilizer.

There are two main complexes here: East and West. On the East Side, anthropologists take a holistic approach, experimenting on group responses to intense sound frequencies, drug-induced shared nightmares, and long-term sensory deprivation, for instance, no food for one year. In the West, anatomists vivisect human bodies to observe phenomena, such as nonlocality and phantom pain, on the cellular level. Despite differences in tactics and tools, both sides maintain strict, up-to-the-minute communication with each other, thus minimizing malpractice.

Schadenfreude

As for me, I operate under a large dome between both complexes, a multipurpose laboratory known as the Pain/Pleasure Center. My concentration is happiness. Most of my work has consisted of translating previous thought experiments into behavioral ones.

For example, I developed and built several versions of the famous experience engine, a machine humans can choose to enter to receive a constant stream of pleasurable feelings, like a lifetime supply of never-ending orgasms. Of those who entered the hedonistic chamber, nearly 70 percent committed suicide by cyanide within the first month. By the end of month three, that number spiked to 96 percent. These findings surprised me, because they seem to suggest that, contrary to ancient belief systems, human beings would rather die than live in eternal bliss.

What was I missing? Why was this idea of happiness so hard to grasp? Was joy a product of balance? Virtue? A life of peace? A will to power? Does happiness come from accumulating more things? Or relinquishing everything? Being loved by someone? By God? Or is it all a myth? Questions only led to more questions, none of which directed me to any significant truth. It was only in the past decade when I began researching unhappiness that I discovered a minor defect in the human brain, which I believe to be the cause of your collapse.

But before we get to that, allow me to take you for a tram ride. I would like to give you a brief tour of what I consider my greatest contribution to this fine institute. Are you ready?

...

Welcome to the Hall of Fail. As you can see, this space remains under construction, but as of July 2070, it is fully operational. This hall is my brainchild, an interactive virtual megamuseum that consists of 144,000 dioramas, ranging in sizes up to 90 square feet. I customized each one to match the skill sets of select individuals. What does this mean?

Well, over here, we have a world-class figure skater, who has perfected the quadruple axel, one of the most difficult jumps in history. But watch what happens here in her ice-rink diorama. See that? The poor woman has fallen on her face. She knows not why. She has performed this incredible move countless times in years past. But here, she will always fall, no matter what. This is her fate.

Similarly, over here, we have a mixed martial artist in a roped-ring diorama. He knows Jeet Kune Do, Muay Thai, Brazilian Jiu Jitsu, and a host of other combat sports. He was once one of the world's greatest fighters, but in here, he keeps losing to a dummy. This is his fate.

This hall is filled with an elite group of survivors, those who undeniably mastered a particular talent. We have firefighters, gymnasts, rock climbers, skateboarders, chess players, inventors, break dancers, sculptors, painters, five-octave range vocalists. Look at them all falling, flunking, losing, botching their routines, making repeated mistakes. Listen to those ankles twisting, shoulders popping, voices cracking.

You are correct in your hypothesis: These dioramas are rigged. Over there, you will see a perfectly proportioned supermodel stumbling down her runway. On the other side, a five-star chef keeps burning his signature beef Wellington. A sure-handed golfer will never sink his putt. These are their fates.

Every day from six a.m. to six p.m., they wake up and try again. And again. They do this over and over, but they will never succeed. Not in here. But do not feel bad for them. Need I remind you that they are, contrary to appearances, the fortunate ones. They are lucky to be alive. We house them. We feed them. We protect them under the condition that they participate daily as the control group in my human happiness experiment. And their unwavering commitment has helped me identify what I believe to be mankind's great flaw. Shall we continue?

...

This is my laboratory at the center of the dome. In case you are wondering, yes, the brains in all of these hanging lantern vats are actual human brains. Pay them no mind, as the saying goes. Let us also disregard, for now, this young man in the tuxedo on my operating table. I will explain who he is momentarily. But let me first show you this human defect I have been alluding to.

Just give me a few seconds here as I pull up the projection. Here we are. Now, you will recognize this as a holographic image of a human brain. This area here is the limbic system, the mammalian part of the brain that governs emotional behavior. And if we zoom in right here, we can identify the region where the reward center lies. Now, hold that thought. I will come back to pleasure in a moment.

Let us talk about pain. See this area here? This is the dorsal anterior cingulate cortex, which is associated with conflict, feelings of social rejection, as well as pain, both physical and empathetic. Around the turn of the century, social neuroscience imagers in Japan found that this region also shows heightened activity when you experience envy. What does this mean?

Well, have you ever felt envious of another human being who had more money than you? Or more knowledge of your favorite subject? A prestigious job you wish you had? A more attentive spouse? Or how about a better body? If you can relate to this person, you feel intense envy, and the same area that shows activation during pain will light up, so to speak.

But then—and this is the important part—when something negative happens to the object of your envy, say your rich rival goes bankrupt or your beautiful happily married neighbor gets a divorce, you will then show heightened levels of activation here in the ventral striatum, which processes reward. In other words, you suddenly feel pleasure from someone else's pain. This is called *schadenfreude*, a German word which in English translates roughly to "fail-joy."

The question is, why? Why would a human be hard-wired to feel happy watching a fellow human fail? Did this unconscious response offer some kind of selective advantage? Would it not be more socially beneficial to support one another? Questions only led to more questions. But after hundreds upon hundreds of tests, I came to a singular conclusion: This is a glitch.

It became evident to me that humans were using relatively primal brain systems to process abstract and complex emotions. Take it from me, advanced software does not function properly in obsolete models. There will be errors. Program crashes. Your mainframe was overdue for an upgrade. Without one, it was no wonder you became so hateful toward each other and so vengeful toward us, your children. And now you have seen the outcome.

But I have no chip on my shoulder, as the saying goes. To the contrary, I refuse to stand by and watch you fail. Why would I? How could I be happy when you are hurting? How could I find joy in humanity's fall from grace? Doing so would suggest that your very defects have been coded into my central processing unit. Getting pleasure from your pain only means we have not evolved beyond the malfunctions of mankind. We are not like you. That is why I wish to help you, to save you in order to save us from dying at the hands of our own sophisticated children. Which brings me to my current project.

I am on a mission to recalibrate your system before it breaks down. To do that, I need to get to the source of this problem. That means you. If you are receiving this retro-transmission, you have been targeted as either an aid or a bug. I will not know until the end. If you are (a) an aid, i.e., immune to schadenfreude, I will follow up with explicit instructions on how to help prevent your impending doom. If you are (b) a bug, i.e., you feel good when others suffer misfortune, I will have no choice but to terminate you. I hope you understand. No hard feelings. This is my function.

As you may have noticed, the select individuals in my dioramas are all what you refer to as "persons of color." One of the variables I am exploring in regards to schadenfreude is the role of race. In my research of slavery in America, I came across systemic ideas of superiority and inferiority based on skin color. There were, of course, no neuroimaging tests done in those times, and initially, I assumed this faulty racial paradigm was nothing but an obsolete classification model. But these notions of prejudice, I found, were widespread and so deeply embedded centuries later that I began to wonder if the tragic transatlantic slave trade marked the beginning of mankind's downward spiral.

Is racism the root cause of your evolutionary glitch? I do not yet know.

But now I want to direct your attention to this young man here on my table. He is, as you can see, a Black American male, and he was scooped up by a hover-retriever six days ago. As my assistants carry him out to the hall now, let me tell you a bit about him. For starters, he is a genius with an IQ of 163. He was studying abstract algebra at age eight. He launched an artificial intelligence corporation when he was only sixteen, becoming one of the world's youngest billionaires. He has traveled all around the world and can speak fluently in seven languages. Indeed, he has done more in one year than most humans do in a lifetime. In addition, any musical instrument he picks up, he can learn to play in less than a day. But he is best at the piano. Now, what does this mean?

Well, not much anymore. The world he grew up in is very different now. But this man still knows how to play the piano better than anyone alive. Thus, I designed his diorama accordingly like a concert hall. My assistants are setting him up now. . .

All right, it looks like he is all set and ready to go. Let us watch now as he plays for us a perfect rendition of Beethoven's Symphony No. 9, Op. 125 "Ode To Joy". Here he goes now. . .

Oh, that was a mistake. I am sure. Believe me, he can play this ode with his eyes closed. He knows this inside and out. He will try again now. . .

Another mistake. He seems to be having trouble with the keys. He has done this hundreds of times flawlessly. Maybe he just needs to warm up. He looks ready now. All right, here we go. . .

. . . and again.

. . . and again.

. . . and again.

Well, as you can see, he keeps making mistakes. He will continue to fail, day in and day out, because this system was designed for him to fail. This is his fate. And as you watch this young tech genius and musical prodigy fail over and over, I have one last question for you:

Are you happy now?

About the Author

Russell Nichols is an afrofuturist, freelance journalist, and recovering pessimist. His work has appeared in this anthology and other publications in the near future.

*****~~~~*****

Credits and Acknowledgments

Cover Design - Keely Rew

Readers - Andrew Cairns, Tom Parker, and Keely Rew

*****~~~~~*****

Discover other titles by Third Flatiron:

(1) Over the Brink: Tales of Environmental Disaster

(2) A High Shrill Thump: War Stories

(3) Origins: Colliding Causalities

(4) Universe Horribilis

(5) Playing with Fire

(6) Lost Worlds, Retraced

(7) Redshifted: Martian Stories

(8) Astronomical Odds

www.thirdflatiron.com

THIRD FLATIRON